Jay L. MacDonald is a former award-winning United Press International wire service reporter who checked out of the news mainstream and into the heady world of 'Key Weird' to pursue fiction. He lived in a dilapidated Cuban rooming house, worked days as a hired worker, and spent nights writing in Key West's most notorious watering holes. Since 2000, he has served as an online freelance feature writer and author interviewer for popular dot-coms Bankrate, BookPage, CreditCards and Montana Press, as well as the Sunday Books Editor for the Fort Myers (Fla.) News-Press daily newspaper, which spawned his Austin Macauley nonfiction debut, "Crazy from the Heat: Fun in the Sun with 35 Florida Authors."

To my adventurous wife Kate and the unforgettable years
we spent living in and loving the Florida Keys.

Jay L. MacDonald

THE LAST TRUE BLONDE

AUSTIN MACAULEY PUBLISHERS™
LONDON · CAMBRIDGE · NEW YORK · SHARJAH

Ordering Information
Quantity sales: Special discounts are available on quantity purchases by corporations, associations, and others. For details, contact the publisher at the address below.

Publisher's Cataloging-in-Publication data
MacDonald, Jay L.
The Last True Blonde

ISBN 9798886932218 (Paperback)
ISBN 9798886932225 (Hardback)
ISBN 9798886932232 (ePub e-book)

Library of Congress Control Number: 2023906985

www.austinmacauley.com/us

First Published 2023
Austin Macauley Publishers LLC
40 Wall Street, 33rd Floor, Suite 3302
New York, NY 10005
USA

mail-usa@austinmacauley.com
+1 (646) 5125767

Table of Contents

Chapter 1
Somebody's Girl

I was making fast friends with the Tallahassee twins when a call came through to the Afterdeck Bar at Louie's Backyard. I unraveled myself from their suntanned young arms and caromed my way to the wait station. Niño the bartender salvaged a perfectly good import from a dozing drunk and slid it down to me. I held the bottle up to a tiki torch. Satisfied that it had not been touched, I nodded thanks to my Cuban friend, downed half of it, then lit a cigarette.

"Jack Dodge." I blew the match out into the receiver.

"If you're buying your own at Louie's, I must be paying you too damn much." I could barely hear Peterson's gravelly baritone over the midnight bar noise.

"Who's dead?" I asked, uninterested. I was off. Some would say permanently.

"Jesus, Jack, doesn't a person get a little foreplay anymore?"

I winked at the twins.

"All right, Chief. Who's dead, *punkin*?"

"Nice of you to ask. White female, mid-20s. Drove a delivery truck down from Dade every week, magazines and newspapers. Didn't make her delivery this time. They found most of her at 45, foot of the bridge."

Everything was mile-marker numbers in the Keys. Pete was at 48, Marathon, in the Middle Keys. I sat at ground zero, end of the line, Key West.

"Tucked and rolled?" The usual MO around here.

"Maybe. But Fink's never seen one like this. Thinks you ought to take a look before he gets started."

"Where's Nash?"

"Still at the scene."

"Do any of you know what time it is, Chief?"

"Time for a cup of the brown stuff, Jack."

I took an intentionally noisy draw from the beer and wiped my face with the rough side of my hand. To say I'd had plans for later was an understatement. The twins, either one of them, were the kind of girls who could put a man on soft food for a week.

"OK," I said at last, "I'm there."

I walked a crooked line back to the table with the bad news. Ordinarily I would have tried to buy time, but not with these two. I knew full well it would take me half an hour just to pedal to the morgue and see what Fink had and I wasn't that pretty or that glib to make it worth their wait. I had no choice but to throw this night back, maybe catch up with them later in the week. After all, it was only Monday.

Hemingway Days, I muttered, saddling up my old Cuban special and pointing it toward the county morgue. For every welcome specimen like the twins who come down to Key Weird for the annual week-long celebration, there are a dozen lowlifes, each bringing his weight in stupidity, greed, violence and, worst of all, work into my life.

Years ago, the local C of C types came up with the idea of an official birthday party for Papa as a way to pump more business into July, the hottest month down here, and hence the nadir of the off-season. Over time, the old man's likeness spread far and wide, thanks to souvenir Sloppy Joe's Saloon tee shirts and later Hemingway Days merchandise, establishing the island's most famous literary barfly as the patron sinner for the southernmost rock in the United States. Quite appropriately, the week preceding the writer's July 21st birthday had become a sweaty drunken bacchanalia that somehow managed to combine a billfish tournament, a literary competition, an arm-wrestling gruntfest and a Papa look-alike contest.

I helped judge the look-alike contest last year and had been shamed into doing it again this year by the old man's granddaughter, Lorian. My grandfather knew the old guy and our families go back. Devoting a couple midsummer evenings to free beer at Sloppy Joe's was my one and only act of civic consciousness—or, if last year is any indication, unconsciousness.

In theory, Hemingway Days should have been embraced by the island's demimonde, the night people, my people. They value a good party above all else. And it would have been, too, had it been carried off with even a hint of subtlety, whimsy, style or taste. Sadly, Papa Week never amounted to much more than a thinly disguised frat party with literary pretensions, serving the singular purpose of pouring as much beer as possible into the visiting Goths. Had old Ern not already done so, a glimpse at the sorry scene these out-of-town rubes created with the pastimes he loved surely would have prompted him to load up the old twelve-gauge.

Ed Fink was a patient man, but a practical one, too. His attention to detail was legendary and many a case had been successfully closed thanks to the precision with which he practiced his ghoulish craft. However, when forensics were not likely to affect the outcome, the Monroe County medical examiner was not averse to leaving a corpse *in refrigeratum* for days at a time while he pursued the wily bonefish, whose presence among the mangrove flats of the lower Keys he considered nothing less than a personal affront. On these occasions, even Pete was inclined to look the other way. It was even rumored, though never proved, that Chief had actually covered for the absent Fink a time or two when outside jurisdictions called in for autopsy results.

Ed Fink was a disciplined man with a fish problem, was all.

Meetings like these were rare, especially on my half of the clock. Fink was a family man, worked a day shift, belonged to Rotary, Kiwanis, the yacht club. A real citizen. I lived a bachelor's life on the night side and belonged to nothing.

"You've made some undeserving bozos at the Backyard very happy tonight," I said as I entered his stainless-steel sanctum.

I've experienced plenty of the horrors of violent death and never let much of it get inside me, but little things about Fink's Sinks gave me the creeps, particularly the postcards neatly taped above his desk and the small radio he kept tuned to the easy listening station.

Ed looked up from his paperwork and dropped his little half-lenses, leaving them dangling from a chain around the collar of his crisp white lab coat.

"Jack," he mewed, with the same false delight one uses with a petulant child.

The far two stainless drain tables were dark. The closest one, on which a small body was draped with a white sheet, was alive with examination lights. I could smell that strange minty antiseptic scent I'd come to associate with death and work. It covered a multitude of far more offensive odors.

"When did she roll in?"

"A family from Atlanta found her when they stopped to take some sunset shots at the bridge. Dog goes nuts, the father investigates, welcome to the Keys, folks. Chief called me just after ten. Body arrived around midnight."

"Truck?"

"Still there, taped shut. Loo figures you'll meet her for breakfast. She'll have snaps by then."

Lieutenant Sarah Nash, out of the Marathon shop. Grisly photos and Danish.

The coroner drew the sheet off the body magician-style as Dionne Warwick asked what do you get when you fall in love? Nash's crew had bagged and tagged the victim's garments, then sent her to Fink much as she'd come into this world, with one notable exception.

I lit a cigarette and slowly circled the table, surveying the damage.

Fink shot me a disapproving look and continued: "They ID'd her as Martina Orlovsky, twenty-four. Resided in

Kendall. Struggling musician. Right-handed, apparently." He picked up her lifeless left wrist and showed me her short nails and blue calluses. "A guitar was in the back of the truck. They found her bound with sixty-pound test."

I acknowledged the deep impressions left by the fishing line.

"You should quit smoking, Jack."

"It's on my list."

"Just from a preliminary examination, I would put the time of death at mid-afternoon. She was in that truck in some heat for several hours. I'll know more from the gut contents and tox screen."

"What about sex?" My drunken nod to Fink's professional wit.

"Thanks, I'm good." Bada bing. "Loo tells me she was fully clothed. I'll know more after the exam. There are signs of a struggle, but she didn't put up much of a fight, or didn't get a chance to. Preliminary indications are there was no sex involved, although I won't be able to rule out oral for obvious reasons."

I squinted through smoke, conceding that point. The victim's head was gone. Severed. A clean removal.

Another lap around the table didn't make things any clearer. Most of an otherwise healthy girl lay dead on a stainless-steel cutting board, bound, beheaded and left to eternity in the back of a delivery truck at the foot of Seven Mile Bridge. Cause of death TBD, although loss of a certain red liquid would have to be a prime contender.

I leaned over the headless neck for a closer look. "What do you make of this?" I pointed with my cigarette.

He gave me a scornful look and gently pushed me back. "I'll study some tissue samples and narrow the field for you."

Fink began preparing the tools of his trade, humming along with Dionne.

"You going to listen to that while you cut her up?" I asked.

"You going to watch?"

I tossed my smoke into the floor drain.

"I'll see you later, Eddie. Call it in to Nash, huh?"

"You got it."

Chapter 2
M

Someday will come. I'm sure of it. I will happen upon it, or I will cause it to happen upon me, or in my least favorite scenario it will simply happen to me unawares. I will recognize the moment by its correct proportion of sun to blood to coral dust, and in that instant, I will receive the knowledge: I will understand why I lost M.

Does it matter that I know this day will come? I don't think so. They say it all becomes clear when we die anyway. I feel some measure of envy that M. is now just watching me play out my cards in her regard, knowing the outcome already.

The cormorants and pelicans feasted on mullet fry as I opened the door to another blinding sunrise on Houseboat Row.

Our merry band of squatters has been clinging barnacle-like to the southeastern shore of the island for decades now, braving hurricanes, developers, city politicos, state envirocrats, low-tide halitosis and the occasional putrid norther from the dump-mound we affectionately call Mount Trashmore.

I inherited the cause, along with the houseboat, from my paternal grandfather, who raised me here as best he could after my birth parents fell hopelessly into their respective addictions. The old boy left this earth drunk and saddled, so it ended happily for him at least. I graduated, drifted upstate and earned college paper, leaving the boat in the hands of various friends and renters while I chased the bad guys in the Metro-Dade game. I finally found the bad guys and lost M. That's when Pete pulled me out and dropped me back aboard the *Jackie Oh!,* a rarer than rare third-generation conch, appropriately lost on this island of lost souls.

Over the years, we fought and fought and fought for Houseboat Row. We were goddamn pigheaded stubborn immovable SOBs, but we only had to gaze across the shallow pass at the glorious mess they were making of Stock Island to find every reason to cling to our little bulkhead. It isn't even the principle of it anymore. We are now an endangered species, fighting for a way of life that is hopelessly beyond explaining to the carpetbaggers and transplanted city dandies at the helm of the island's destiny.

It is with no small irony that they refer to us as conchs; those regal and most tenacious crustaceans are almost gone, too.

We persevered for so long that we are now considered 'colorful', meaning we fit somehow into the latest grand design with which the Economic Development Council hopes to encourage tourism to this rock. So be it. We've managed to survive Disneyfication, with its Margaritaville and Hard Rock Café and Planet Hollywood. We can certainly withstand the invasion of single lens reflex shutters and the whir of foreign camcorders.

Houseboat conchs—the few, the proud, the seriously inebriated. We control our own drunken destiny, such as it is.

I hadn't seen an actual morning-morning for some weeks. You live in one of two time zones in Key West—the tanned, worker-bee day world or the sallow, unsunned, nightclubbing one. I returned home nearly two years ago, shortly after losing M., fully intending to turn in my workmanlike 8-to-5 shift on the dayside and drink myself to death at night. After several unproductive weeks trying that, it was clear to me that the peculiar brand of crime here in the Keys takes place almost entirely after dark. I've been on nights ever since, by choice. Suits my temperament, Pete says. Probably saved my life, too, more's the pity.

Jurgen and Horst, the Germans next door, waved as I juggled my briefcase and a mug of joe up the short ramp and onto the salty sediment-covered seat of the Jeep. Healthy guys. I'd known the two previous owners of their houseboat, having slept with the one, a lonely divorcee, during my adolescence, and drank with the other, a retired purser, just prior to his earthly departure. These two are sun worshipping fitness fanatics who share a passion for show tunes that borders on the fanatical. Our paths cross frequently in the clubs. They're of the opinion that any bachelor over 30 is a closet case and they're waiting for me to 'come out'. They've got quite a wait on their hands.

You live on this rock awhile, you get withdrawal symptoms just driving up-island. Key West pulls at you. Not in a good way, like a lover pleading for five more minutes. More like emphysema.

I visit Marathon as little as possible and it's always for the job. Peterson runs the county from there. Says it's a better family town. Nash is one of his best hires, young and bright and spunky, a Metro-Dade refugee like Pete and me. We've looked each other sideways a few times but what would be the point? There are fifty miles and a few years between us. And M. Still, the kid's a nice change of scenery.

I pulled into Pete's spot, not that it mattered, this hour. Fishermen are the only early risers in the Keys. Loo looked good in her crisp, pressed county issue, leaning against a fender. She prefers the dress version. So do I, on her. Sets off those long Creole legs.

"Sick of Sally's, Jack?"

"That'll work," I said.

We rode in her unmarked Crown Vic down US 1 to the popular cop eatery. Nash pulled a handled cardboard box from the trunk. I dragged my overfilled canvas briefcase along. We grabbed a window booth in the back.

The lieutenant produced a stack of color glossies taken from the scene. I rifled through them. Fairly gory stuff, lots of blood turned brown by the time the photog arrived. The victim's clothing, that which hadn't absorbed too much, gave the best description yet of who Martina Orlovsky of Kendall had been in life, a free spirit party girl from the looks of things.

Nash sipped her coffee as I shuffled the prints, comparing this one to that, the way you begin any jigsaw puzzle.

"Pete seen these?" I asked.

"Last night. Before we sent her down to you."

"What's his take?"

Nash tapped one manicured nail on a close-up of the clean cut at the neckline.

"Yeah, that's our problem," I agreed.

The lieutenant pulled a zip-seal bag from her evidence box and handed it to me. The victim's purse. I studied the face on the Florida driver's license, then flipped through the rest. In the money pouch was a cocktail coaster from Billie's, a watering hole in the heart of Old Town Key West. I flipped it. There was another island phone number scrawled on the back. I jotted it down on my pad, then took down the Social Security number, Kendall address and physical description off her license: blue eyes, blond hair, height 5–5, weight 115. Then I took one long last look at the license photo.

"We won't have long on this, Jack. I can drag out the paperwork past the deadline here, but it's going to hit the *Citizen* Thursday or Friday, you know that." The Middle Keys had a weekly newspaper. The *Key West Citizen* was a daily.

"What else we got?"

"Odds and ends. A guitar, makeup case, a few pills, a couple joints."

"The outfit she drove for. Legit?"

"Sure. Mob, but legit enough. Operates out of a warehouse off Calle Ocho." Sarah knew Miami, too. We'd both had the sense to get out. I just made the move a little too late, is all.

"What did Ed come up with?"

"Tox screen was negative. Stomach contained fast food, burger and fries, probably someplace here local. No semen. Struggle was negligible. Loss of blood's his best guess now, judging by what was left in the body. I'd say that squares with what we found in the truck. She may have been struck in the head first. But obviously…"

"Yeah."

"That serration to the neck tissue? It looks like a power saw of some kind to me. He's working on the gauge. Pretty small teeth to the thing, apparently. Could be a rotary saw with a specialized blade, but he won't rule out surgical equipment until he makes the gauge."

"And the family that found her?"

Nash recounted the details of her interview. They had been so shaken up they hadn't even spent a night on the county. Hightailed it upstate in their minivan.

"There was a call, though," she said. "I didn't give it much when it came in because the body hadn't been discovered. A fisherman doing some mooching under the bridge called Marx on the marine band, saying he saw what looked like a holdup, through his binoculars anyway."

"We have a contact on this guy?"

"Name's Drury Treegarten. Owns the *Lotsa Luck*. A local."

The old fisherman held a bait-stained hand to Nash and steadied her as we stepped onboard. The *Lotsa Luck* was an old twin-hull that had seen better days. The morning sun penetrated the bottle-green water clear to the sandy bottom beneath us. You could see grouper and barracuda pass by in the shadow of the bridge pilings. The old man made us comfortable on flotation cushions I wouldn't want to sea-test and offered us thermos coffee. Nash flipped on her tape recorder.

Treegarten said he'd been trying his luck at some mid-afternoon mooching lately, but they weren't biting yesterday. Bored, he started scanning the shore with his binoculars. There he saw a pretty young blonde in short-shorts and halter-top having lunch under a poinciana. He noticed the delivery truck but didn't connect it with the girl at first. He'd been watching her awhile when a shiny black sport utility vehicle coming from the direction of Marathon pulled off the road, kicking up dust, and parked behind the truck.

"First I thought maybe she was expecting someone," he said. "She seemed to know him, the way she greeted him. Fella in his fifties, I'd say. Not tall. Heavy-set maybe. Don't know that he fished but he had the get-up. Khakis. Even the cap. White beard and sunglasses. Yep."

"What then?" Nash asked.

"He and the girl, they talk a little while. Anyway, she gets up and they head over to the old truck. They disappear around the rear of the thing, I can't see them for a long time. Then I seen the feller go and fetch a bag from his rig and head back into the gal's truck and close the back doors there. That's when I called your marine patrol feller. A little while later, I seen his rig pull out and head on over the bridge."

"Did you get a look at his plates?" I asked.

"Never did. They were behind him. Windows were dark, though, if it'll help you."

"How long did you watch them?" Nash asked.

"Oh, I don't know, twenty, thirty minutes tops." The old man eyed his several poles, gently rocking with the stream.

We thanked him and stood up carefully.

"Reckon he robbed her, did he?" he asked.

Nash looked at me.

"Yeah," I said. "Something like that."

Chapter 3
Discretion

The Chief was in when we returned. Nash made a beeline to her desk, wrapping up the call on her flip phone with one hand, dialing out on her office line with the other. I entered Pete's glass case.

"I don't have a good feeling about this one," I told him.

"Yeah, good one." He didn't even look up.

I poured us some joe, squinting through one last drag on my JIC.

"Reminds me of something you said when you were sweet-talking me with all the reasons I should take this job. Remember?"

He leaned back, pushed his god-awful horn rims back up that big black broken nose and blinked at me through them.

"Jesus, Jack, there were so many shovelfuls."

I stubbed my cigarette out in his ashtray. "And I quote, 'You'll see more body parts than bodies in Key West.'"

He grunted, nodding at his own prescience. "Not exactly what I meant, though." His eyes wandered back to a hopelessly thick stack of reports. "What's the fisherman's story?"

I gave him the short version.

"Circumstantial." His worse profanity.

"Suspect did enter and leave the truck with a bag of some kind. I'm thinking tools for the job. Handy for carrying a fresh head, too. Beyond that, the description matches a hundred local fishermen, right down to the SUV."

"Any more on the girl?"

"Nash is working the phones up-island. Newsstands, the magazine outfit, fast food joints, the girl's family."

I absently thumbed through the duty book. It seemed like another life when I made those same routine calls, broke up the same domestic fights, treated seriously the everyday infractions even God overlooks these days.

"Pete, you sure you want to put me on this?" I hardly seemed the best candidate anymore. Hell, I was more likely to be in his duty book these days.

He took off his service specs and massaged the bridge of his nose. He knew why I was asking.

"Jack, how long have we known each other, Miami and here? Nine, ten years? Didn't I pull your crazy ass out of the crowd and bring you up? And you made me proud, you sure did. First Vice. Then Narco. Then the game. You were the best, Jack. Still would be, too."

I started to speak but he stopped me with that rib-roast hand of his.

"Now it's true I can't begin to know how much M. meant to you. And I can't bring her back, either. But I know how much watching you work means to *me*, and *you* there's something I can do about, at least as long as you're drawing a county paycheck. You want to drink yourself six feet under, that's your business. But until you do, you ain't going to deny me the pleasure of watching a born natural show us how to do this job. Who knows, you might even come to like it again, you sober up enough to give yourself a chance. I'm sorry about M. You know that. But joining her ain't the answer."

This old ground was pretty well plowed between us. Work or don't work, kill or be killed. I abstained from caring. I sometimes think Pete is the last one left who believes that the good guys win and the bad guys lose. Or cares.

I acknowledged my new assignment with a two-fingered salute and headed for the door.

"Oh Dodge. You are aware there's a little something called Hemingway Days going on down there this week?" Sometimes Pete liked to synchronize our realities, just to be on the safe side.

"Tell me. Lorian's got me judging again. Just what I need's a twist-o this week."

"Then I don't have to give you the business sensitivity speech, right? You're going to be discreet, like we agreed?"

Pete had busted his considerable hump to mend fences with the EDC in the wake of his predecessor's Wild West brand of justice. He didn't need any loose cannons going off during major-money weekends.

"Consider me Miss Manners."

Pete rolled his eyes as I walked out.

"Yeah, Miss *Bad* Manners with a .45," he mumbled.

Crime scenes, especially homicides, always leave plenty of solid leads for the taking. Trouble is, we're just too thick-headed to see them. Most violent crimes, armed robberies, rapes, assaults, they scan like works in progress;

some things happened leading up to the act, some things will occur following it. Like walking in on the middle of a play. Homicides have a different feel altogether. Everything you need to know about a murder has already taken place. Murder scenes are end scenes, like walking in at the end of the third act, right before they drop the curtain. In some cases, the murderer will kill again, but don't bet on it. Ninety-nine percent of the time, murder scenes scan in only one direction—backward.

Two lab rats were taking latents off the rear loading doors when I arrived. I ducked my head inside the slaughter car. Shafts of morning sunlight revealed an explosion of blood, on walls, ceiling, seatbacks, and across a jury-rigged canvas partition. Spatters of liquefied tissue clung to the metal cargo hold like death itself. Stacks of tabloid newsprint were saturated where the corrugated steel flooring had channeled the blood. The coppery tang was fast giving way to the rotting stench of carnage. Flies were gathering from miles around.

I dug into my jeans for a small penknife and cut the heavy plastic crossbinding on a bundle of supermarket tabloids. I rifled them along the spine side until I felt a difference in the thickness of the newsprint. I pulled the stack apart to reveal a second stack of a thinner publication. I pulled one from the bundle. A black-and-white, hard-core pornography rag. Stroke books, a quaint sidelight of the mob-run magazine distribution industry in the Southeast, were still a moneymaker despite the widespread availability of full color video coupling and Internet porn. Maybe they bought them for the articles. I rolled it up and put it in my back pocket.

One of the lab rats, his hair netted, face covered in a scented surgeon's mask, handed me two photocopies. One showed a patterned shoe print that would likely match the sandals found on the victim. I flipped to the other, a larger sole with wide parallel bands running across the instep and repeated again toward the heel. He motioned to his partner, who put down a blood-spattered *Sports Illustrated* and, turning his back to me, lifted his left shoe to reveal the same pattern I had been studying. Tanned, stitched-leather construction shoes, the kind that come with a steel reinforced toe and soles designed for traction on slippery wet surfaces.

I checked out the cab. The key was still in the ignition, a tattered cardboard tag with a worn number 49 in felt marker hanging from it. I flipped the card over. It read PNB Newsstand Services, now sun-faded gray on a light blue background. Using my handkerchief, I turned the ignition. The truck didn't start, but the radio did. I recognized the station, a Key West signal. The boys next door played it constantly. I switched it off and patted down the glove box, under the seat and over the visor, just habit.

The lab rats were finishing up stowing their powders and potions into the mobile crime unit.

"These mine?" I asked, waving the shoe prints.

"Take 'em, Jack."

"By the way, did you get the cab?"

They looked at each other. "Yeah. Steering wheel, door handle."

"Look, I know it's hot and it stinks, but do me a favor, would you, and dust the radio?"

Chapter 4
Cold Storage

When I got home, it was after one, hot as blazes, and the answer machine was blinking. First up was Lorian. I skipped it. Next was Jonah. I listened a moment then skipped it. Nash came on.

"Jack, it's Sarah. Twelve-thirty. I'm at Dante's Booksellers. One of the regulars here knew her a little. Next of kin, parents in Broward, have been notified. Homestead's on it. I should have their report this afternoon. They'll e-mail scans from Kendall. So far nothing from our calls to Miami. You can reach me on my cellular."

Next up, the Tallahassee twins. I listened with interest to their plans for the evening. They seemed to be taking a Sherman's-march approach to their exploration of Key Weird nightlife.

Then Lorian again, about the contest. I let her give me the details as I struggled out of my sweaty oxford and cranked the rickety A/C window unit. Friday and Saturday nights, nine o'clock on, Sloppy's. Something about new judges, something about behaving better than last year, let's have dinner soon, love ya.

I'd been putting off calling Rick Michaels, my preppy young counterpart at Key West PD, despite our agreement to share information on possible suspects on the run, bodies in the mangroves, that sort of thing. Marathon meant nothing to Rick, strictly out of jurisdiction, somebody else's problem, in this case mine. On the other hand, he might be persuaded to press his bike soldiers into service if I volunteered details about the head. Michaels had a taste for cop-show violence and always seemed to act a little more civil toward me when I fed his monkey.

I dialed his direct line.

"Richard Michaels." Straight from the cop-show home course.

"Christ, you're in."

"Hey, what's new with County Jack?" Always the diminutive with him.

"Been up-island. Caught a big fish in Marathon, right under the bridge."

"Anyone I'll miss?" Trying to be flip, but he was listening. Hard.

I gave him the full bloody account.

Michaels works three to five legit homicides a year. The rest of his job involves processing ODs, suicides and accidentals—drownings, geek sex gone bad, man verses machine, alcoholic spontaneous combustion, or various combinations thereof. Hell, at his age, who wouldn't covet the kind of caseload I had? Sometimes I try to console him, lend him as much of a sympathetic ear as I've got in me, just to try to break through the animosity between us. But Rick, you have all the crazies here, I assure him. It's not your fault they always dump the bodies up-island.

"I'm thinking we could use some help locating the black SUV," I said in summary. "Interested?"

"You think it was some battery-operated job or did he run it off the lighter?" He was still rolling around in the back of that damn delivery truck.

"Never know. Somebody this twisted, where else is he going to go but Key West?"

"You think?"

"Probably here already, cruising right down Duval with that nasty Black and Decker of his."

"All right, Jack, look, I'll put a couple bike officers on it, see what we can find. But you have to promise to bring me in this time." I'd neglected to uphold my end of these deals a time or two. Swingin' Dick never forgets to remind me.

"You know I love your company. And you dance exquisitely, too."

"You think?"

Actually, he did. But not with me.

"Let me know when you find the damn thing, OK?"

"Want help with the head?"

"Yeah, that'd be good. Call if one turns up."

I vaguely recall being his age, another life ago. All training-school bull semen, drunk on myself. Time takes care of that, if a bullet doesn't. Experience burns up enthusiasm like a flame eats the wick of a candle. Mine blew out entirely when I lost M.

I fished my Big Chief pad out of the rubble-pile I call my briefcase. I didn't carry the monster case much anymore because I never seemed to find time to clean it out and it was now too big and bulky to cope with. I flipped to the phone number the victim had written on the back of the coaster from Billie's and dialed it. No one answered, not even a machine. I dialed my liaison at the phone company and cross-checked the number. He turned up a business listing: Puss 'n' Boots. I passed on the address. I knew the place.

One last errand before crashing. I drove to the victim's intended destination, Key West Cold Storage, a huge concrete-block warehouse on Trumbo Road. Inside was dark and cool, the clammy white walls now faded to a dishwater gray. An annoying buzzer sounded as I entered, summoning a young Bahamian woman from a small windowed office.

"Can I help you?" she asked cautiously, on edge.

I showed her my badge and ran down the short version. She showed me her magnificent white teeth and explained she was a temp, called in mid-morning when the man who was supposed to be there had not reported for work. She was met at the door by several angry fishermen. What a day it had been, searching for keys, searching for everything.

"You mind if I take a look in back?" I asked her.

She laughed that wonderfully rich island laugh, relieved that I wasn't another angry angler. "You can do that, but you'll have to find the lights, sir. Even the fishermen, they had to bring their own back there. They didn't like that."

After several fruitless minutes of searching for the power box myself, I gave up and returned to the Jeep for my squad light and my .45.

The darkness smelled like low tide and urine as I stepped into the dank expanse and swept my beacon around the place. The cold storage—to call it dry storage would get you laughed at in this town—had been home to a succession of failed enterprises through the years. The remains of those broken dreams, old facades, false ceilings, decorative scenery and neon beer signs, were suspended overhead, up between the exposed ventilation ducts and rusted florescent fixtures, giving the place a creepy backstage feeling.

I wandered into the center of the darkness, shining my squad light along row upon row of locked hurricane cages filled with fishing skiffs, lobster pots and the usual bric-a-brac people store for reasons of their own: stuffed animals, German cuckoo clocks, accounting textbooks and the like. I never saw much use in keeping more than you need to live so I'm no expert on what compels people to stockpile boxes of copper wire or Mason jars. They just do.

In the center of the great expanse was the cold storage area. I drew my .45 from beneath my shirt and threw the door open. The refrigerated entry room served as a kind of insulating buffer between three walk-in freezers and the musty stench of the warehouse proper. The wall switch inside the door worked fine as little dim bulbs cast an adequate light from their rusty cages. I entered the freezer compartments carefully. In the first two, locked wire bins contained all matter of frozen fish, fowl and game, most of it wrapped in butcher paper, some in cellophane, some just lying there exposed. The third freezer contained larger storage units behind solid locked doors. There were years of bloodstains on the frozen concrete floors. Some of the big units were bent from prying. I flipped the lights out and tucked my gun away as I left.

At the rear of the warehouse was an old commercial boat launch, long ago abandoned to rust and decay. Flies hovered lazily in thin shafts of summer sunlight streaming through the gaps in the double wooden swing doors. I walked a few steps down the ramp beneath the old roller hoist. Water no longer reached into the old launch. Out back was probably coral-rock fill now.

To the right of the ramp was an antique diesel fuel tank, and beyond it stood an old walk-in block-ice machine. Before the advent of onboard marine refrigeration, block-ice makers had been a fixture of every commercial dock in these parts. Lots of smaller operators still preferred block ice to the upkeep of a reefer. Then again, some of those guys would still have iceboxes back at their mobile homes if they could get delivery. Same guys who stockpile cuckoo clocks, I bet.

I could hear the compressor of the block-ice maker as I came closer. The heavy white enamel coating had given way to rust here and there, but the old workhorse seemed to be humming along pretty well for its age.

How long had it been since I'd last seen this block-ice machine? I couldn't remember, but it had figured in my earliest fishing memories, mixed in there with the smells of cigarette smoke, black coffee, bait shrimp and outboard exhaust. Grandpa Max would have me take the old metal cooler down to the end where the stainless-steel chute, exactly the width of an ice block, comes out. I'd listen for him sorting through his pockets until he found a quarter, then he'd wink down to me at my end and say, "Hands clear, boy," and then he'd drop the two bits in. I loved to hear the machine rumble as the huge cube skidded down the wheeled conveyors and out the metal flume, crashing in all its icy thunder against that catcher. I had to use my sweatshirt to get a handle on it and wrestle it into our cooler because I wasn't strong enough or tall enough to make much use of the huge tongs.

The beast had a dollar-bill feeder now, set right in at the same end as the catcher. And there was a fancy nylon sling attachment that would have come in handy years ago.

A buck. What the hell. Old time's sake. I fished through my outriggers for a dollar, aimed the squad light at the slot and carefully fed the bill into the sadly contemporary-sounding feeder until it took. But there followed the same old hum, the dull clunk of the release lever, and that glorious racket of ice skidding along steel, just as I remembered from my boyhood.

The cold cube was on its way, coming nearer and nearer. I held the squad light steady on the chute, waiting for the chips to fly. The block-ice rumble finally reached me, the rubber door flew open, and chips scattered, stinging my bare shins and staining my salt-cured topsiders with a spray of frozen blood.

There in the trap, eyes and mouth wide open in an expression of unspeakable horror, was the cleanly severed head of Martina Orlovsky, suspended in bloody ice.

This was going to be Swingin' Dick's lucky day.

Chapter 5
Breakfast at Billie's

The hour of sack time I attempted before twilight was filled with memories of M. They seem to blot out everything, even frozen heads. Even sleep.

Billie's was quiet. I brought Jonah up to speed over coffee and huevos rancheros. Outside, the sunset was turning Old Town from sepia to brick red, giving our faces more color than they deserve.

We'd taken to meeting semi-regularly for breakfast at sundown, an informal arrangement that evolved out of dire circumstances on my part and a good measure of stubborn loyalty on his. There had been a lot of alcohol and loneliness that first year without M. There still was, after nearly two. But Jonah and his friends know the territory well and somehow managed to keep me alive through it. Miraculously, between Jonah's persistence and Pete's patience, I'd survived intact my first year without M., employed, shaky, but still technically counted in the census. We differ on the wisdom of that, whether it is cruel to be kind. Still, it's not overstating matters to say that Jonah saved my life. So far. More's the pity.

My diet still weaves drunkenly past the five major food groups, my bar tab still runs neck and neck with my paycheck, and the hole where M. used to be still twists my guts and wrecks what little sleep I bother to attempt. But I'm here. I suppose I should feel more grateful than I do.

Everyone in Key Weird is running from something: ex-husbands, ex-wives, crazy mothers, abusive fathers, the taxman, the policeman, the hitman, the big four-oh, the world at large, the voices in their head, a great potential. Or a memory. Pick one or more. Like the tee shirts say, "See the Lower Keys on your hands and knees." Or another one, "Key West—I've been all the way." Most of us recognize that this is the end of the road in more ways than one.

Billie's, once a favorite haunt, no longer opens its arms to me. During my extended lost weekend, I'd been 86'd from here three times, all for very good reasons, I'm told. I would talk my way back in with each new bartender, only to cuss, spit and fight my way back out again. We finally reached an uneasy truce: no food, no booze. So I eat. Or order, anyway.

The night manager was a block of woman named Lulu. I was certain she would be of no intentional help. She was one of the tribe I call the yellow-eyed. Self-serving and spiteful by nature. She loathed me in particular and took her time finding time to submit to my questions.

I handed her two computer printouts, snapshots scanned by the Homestead lab rats and e-mailed to me late in the day from the victim's apartment.

"Recognize her, Lulu?"

"Should I?" She was sweating through a bar shirt that struggled to contain her.

"She's a musician. You've got an open-mike here Monday nights, right?"

"Yeah."

"Five-five. Slim. Drove a magazine truck down from Dade once a week."

"Good for her. I'm off Mondays."

Our waitress, a toned young party girl named Brett, reached for the printouts.

"I know her, Jack. She played here last week and a few times before that. Calls herself Marty Orleans. Stage name, I think. Her hair's different now, though. More of a Dixie do, rodeo queen look. Plays mostly country stuff."

Lulu gave me a look. I excused her. She huffed past Brett.

"I don't know about a truck. She used to come in with a local guy. I've seen him around. Bahamian. The last couple times, though, she was with two women. Girl's girls, you know."

I jotted down their physical descriptions.

"Did you talk to her?"

"Yeah, we talked a little. They sat in my section. Ran a tab, the three of them. I told her I liked her voice. She seemed nice, easy to talk to, you know? But I was getting serious vibes from the other two so I didn't hang out."

"Anything strange about her, vibe-wise?"

Brett propped a tennis shoe against my barstool, pulled her tray against her chest and thought. "I had the feeling she wasn't one of the girls? She didn't seem that way to me? More like a third wheel. But around here, who knows? Right, Jonah?"

"Life is diverse," he agreed, engrossed in the day's crossword puzzle.

"I'm guessing she didn't pick up the tab."

"You would be right, Jack." She scratched out our check. I handed her a twenty and left a ten on her tray.

"What do you remember about the ?" I asked.

"Let's see. Tall. Thin. Wears hats all the time. I think he had a thing for her but she wasn't into that either, from what I could tell. They were just friends, at least to her. He was a sipper. Paid cash. Maybe he drove the truck?"

"You remember anything else about her?"

"She always played pretty early, which is sort of odd. Most of the open-mikers like to play later, more people, better tips. She was always here early, before sunset sometimes. Let's see. She wore cowboy boots. Red ones. With shorts, even. Don't see that much around here."

I asked her to get in touch if any of the other Monday regulars could add to the picture.

"She's in trouble, right?"

"Dead right. You surprised?"

"No. Seemed like trouble was something she was looking for."

I admired Brett's muscle tone as she drifted away. We'd partied together a time or two, back when it was all a blur. She seemed to know me better than I knew her.

"A five-letter word for attractive backside," Jonah said. "Wait, I have it! B-o-o-t-y. Booty."

"Jealous."

Jonah carefully refolded the *Citizen*. "Sounds like we've found our Puss 'n' Boots connection. Assuming I'm invited."

Club Chameleon, the venerable cabaret where Jonah is the headliner, was dark Mondays and Tuesdays, hence they'd become our usual nights to club crawl together. We hadn't been to Puss 'n' Boots recently. Not a place we frequented, for obvious reasons. Still, when whatever stray souls we found ourselves schooling with decided to explore rough trade or girl-girl variety, off to Puss 'n' Boots we'd go. My seriously flawed recollection was that a lot of very suggestive dancing went on there but that they were reasonably tolerant of male customers as long as you kept it in your pants. I was pretty sure I'd never been thrown out of the place, but then I'm not the best one to ask.

We took the back alley to Duval. I'd just placed a fresh cigarette in my mouth and was about to torch it when I froze in my tracks, adrenaline spoiling my largely liquid breakfast. Stepping off the curb a block in front of us was a heavy-set bearded man in khaki exactly matching the description the old fisherman had given me earlier in the day. He wasn't wearing sunglasses, as the sun was well past setting, but I would have bet it was him.

Jonah ceased savoring the unfolding nightlife and looked at me, puzzled.

"That's him! That's the guy we're after!" I whispered, struggling to keep him in sight amid the cattle drive of tourists advancing on us from the Mallory sunset rituals. Jonah held me back, but just.

The suspect crossed Duval, oblivious. Then, to my utter shock, another one appeared, then another, until a merry group of them, all matching the old fisherman's description, stood mingling at the very same curb. When the light changed, they too bellied across Duval in a stampede toward Sloppy's.

"Oh, Christ," I moaned, lighting up.

Jonah cuffed the back of my neck and clicked his tongue scoldingly.

"And they trust you to be a judge," he quipped.

Chapter 6
Puss 'n' Boots

I wrestled the Jeep through the narrow lanes of Old Town, reminiscing with Jonah about lesbian bar fights we'd known. As a cross-dressing heterosexual, Jonah enjoyed a favored-novelty status among the lesbian community. I teased him that he only went that route to lure the stray lambs and bi-girls to hit on him. He never said that it worked, but he never denied it either.

The consolation prize for enduring a summer in Key Weird is finding readily available parking in Old Town. Still, on any evening, it was rare to find a spot directly in front of Puss 'n' Boots. At this hour, the alleyway off Whitehead Street was usually accessible only on foot.

Jonah checked his makeup. I checked my gun.

As we approached the lavender door and awning, no familiar throbbing disco rumble came forth to welcome us. The tiny brass lantern that normally illuminates the character from the children's book was dark. Above the brass door handle was a computer-printed postcard encased in a plastic frame: "Our friends: As you can see, Puss 'n' Boots is closed for the season. Do come back for our grand reopening Halloween eve."

"Probably at the Cape," Jonah sighed dramatically.

As in Provincetown, Cape Cod, aka Key Weird north. Jonah considered all snowbirds an inferior and fickle species, and held their summer refuges in equal disdain. I didn't care for the winter visitors for an altogether different and more selfish reason: they had an annoying habit of getting themselves killed down here, one way or another, thus interrupting my more or less ongoing Happy Hour. Still, they really got under Jonah's skin with their constant recounting of sun-kissed romantic adventures at the Cape, Fire Island or the French Riviera. I think it took every minute of our trance-inducing Key Weird summers to fortify him for the return of the beautiful migrants.

I tried the door. It was unlocked. I knocked. Nothing.

I dug out the Jeep keys and handed them to Jonah.

"Fausto's?" I suggested.

"Cigarettes, I suppose," he huffed, slapping the keys back in my hand. He knew the drill; this investigator works alone. There was a lift to his step as he pumped his way down the alley toward Old Town's only grocery store.

I was inside before the sound of Jonah's heels had faded into the Duval din.

A cigarette machine lighted the dark, narrow entryway. The place smelled of stale beer and a particularly musty perfume I call fat-girl scent. I drew my .45 from beneath my yellow shirt, inhaled, and made a fast crouch spin into the club.

In the half-light of red exit signs, I could see stools stacked along the U-shaped bar, chairs and tables pushed off to one corner of the room. A cluster of furniture and unfamiliar shapes were arranged on the darkened dance floor. Somewhere an icemaker hummed, cubes fell.

I slowly approached the bar. Visually clearing it, I moved with equal caution toward the dance floor. The large shapes turned out to be photography screens, the kind used as backdrops to portraiture. The lower pieces consisted of a futon bed, several pieces of furniture, two freestanding floor lamps and a hefty camera tripod.

The two private rooms in back began to worry me.

I made a quick check of the bar furniture piled in the corner, then worked my way toward the rear. Quickly ducking through a beaded curtain, I entered the dark passage and paused to let my eyes adjust to a smaller, dimmer red exit sign over the back door.

Someone was there. I could sense their presence. In old houses, it's easier to tell, as if the ghosts of the long-dead cigar makers were there motioning you on with a telling glance, a slow nod of a straw hat, a twitch of a pencil-thin moustache over an afterlife café Cubano.

I took several careful steps further into the red din, keeping the unisex restrooms at my back until I faced the two private rooms.

These were the very situations Pete begged me to avoid after losing M. He liked to use words like death wish and suicide, as if he knew anything about them. I've explained to him several times that the hardest thing in the world is to actually get someone to kill you. It's as if they sense it and can't pull the trigger, or they can't believe it and pause just long enough for you to blow a hole the size of a Granny Smith through their upper body. I can't seem to make Pete understand that I'd be in a lot more danger if I actually wanted to live.

I crossed the hallway, pressing my back to the wall next to the first door. With miniscule movements, I turned the door handle until the latch was free. Muscular memory took over as I wheeled into the sitting room, hunched low, ready to exchange fire. None came. What I could see of the bedroom-size space, jammed as it was with a loveseat, sofa, cocktail tables and a wet bar, was empty and unused.

I flattened myself back into the hallway. If someone was waiting behind door number two, I had just lost any remaining element of surprise. I took the knob in a sweaty palm and forced a turn. No dice. Inhaling sharply, I wheeled on the door and kicked it in, following in a crouch.

I didn't have time to look around. Out in the hallway, heavy breathing and the sound of heavier footsteps rushed toward the entrance. I flew through the beaded curtain and drew down on the large figure sprung from the restroom.

"Stop or drop!" I shouted.

She froze.

"Turn now."

A Bahamian woman, twice my width, slowly faced me, holding her chest, wide-eyed, panicked. I lowered the .45 to my side and walked toward her, dragging a pair of stacked chairs behind me. She was terrified, but relieved to sit.

"You smoke?"

She shook her head no, breathless, eyes still wild.

I fished a couple bucks out of my chinos and took my chances with the machine. It had my brand.

"And you would be?" I asked her, wrestling the cellophane.

"Why should I tell you a thing?"

I squinted at her as I lit up. "I have a big gun?" I suggested.

"Althea." She folded her massive arms.

"Name's Jack." I held out my hand. Surprised, she shook it. "Althea what?"

"Danswaller."

"Are you a drinking woman, Althea?" I asked, leaning over the bar, keeping one eye to her.

She glanced toward the door, measuring the distance, then shook her head. I poured myself a half-highball glass of call bourbon and straddled a chair facing her.

"Cheers."

She just looked away.

"Now, Althea, you would be in here because?"

"I work here, cleaning up."

"But they're closed. Says so on the door."

"I check in on the place, you know."

"In the dark?"

"Are you going arrest me?"

"Did you do something wrong?"

"I tell you something, you won't say who told it you?"

"Depends what you tell me."

"My brother, he doesn't come home last night. I fix him dinner, I don't hear from him last night, today. Sometimes he stays here, in back. He does work for them. I come see if I can find him here, that's all. He's not supposed to stay here no more."

"What's his name?"

"Everett. Everett Danswaller."

"And he works here?"

"No more. He work at the big storehouse, down Trumbo."

"Key West Cold Storage?"

"That place."

I smoked, studying her. "Who do you work for here?"

"Two ladies. Miss Jen, Miss Abby."

She provided a reasonable approximation of the couple Brett had described wining and dining Martina Orlovsky at Billie's. She'd been in their employ for two years, through a service.

"How long has Everett worked for them?"

"Since just Christmastime, on and off. Odd jobs mainly. He helped them decorate, for parties and such."

"And they let him sleep here?"

She looked away. "Sometimes they buy him a drink."

"You ever sleep here?"

"Oh no! I've got little ones!"

"And how long has he worked at the cold storage?"

"I think just this year."

"And now he's missing. Has he ever gone missing before?"

"No, he's a good man."

"You got a photo?"

She rummaged through her enormous woven shoulder bag, picked through an overloaded wallet and handed me a dog-eared Sears portrait.

"Does he like his job? At the warehouse?"

"Sure. Good jobs don't fall on us here, you know."

"Did you notice any change in his behavior the past few months?"

Looking away again. "He didn't sleep much, going out with friends in the evening and such. But he earned it, no?"

"Have you ever heard the name Martina Orlovsky?"

She squeezed her enormous upper arms, considering. "I don't know that name."

"How about PNB Newsstand Services? Ever hear of it?"

"P&B, sure."

My puzzled look this time. "How do you know them?"

She gave me a puzzled look back. "P&B," she said, gesturing about her. "It's what they call this. Puss 'n' Boots. I don't know the other, no."

Althea locked the place up. I showed her my badge to cover Pete's butt and offered her a ride. She declined and went tottering off in the direction of Gato Village.

Jonah, arms folded leaning hipshot against the Jeep, gave me a look.

We stopped by Key West PD. Michaels was still at the cold storage, but the shift leader handed me two messages from him.

A bike unit found the SUV, a black Land Rover with Dade plates, abandoned earlier in the day out near Garrison Bight. It had been reported stolen near Gulfstream Park, the horse track north of Miami. Probably an insurance scam. They dusted. No prints so far.

The other message was an e-mail printout of Sarah's report on Marty Orleans that filled in a few more details: Moved in with her parents in Lauderhill after mustering out of the Navy two years ago, made squat playing small clubs around Dade and Broward mostly. The folks knew of several nameless boyfriends, no girlfriends to speak of. First of the year, Marty moved into the Kendall apartment with a guy. Shortly after, she got the delivery job through a regular at a club she was playing. The Marathon bookseller called her a lively little hustler, kind of flirty sometimes, always talking about where she was playing, big plans to be a star. Said she wore a back brace because of the lifting that made her sweat through her halter-tops. Without a bra, it made for a wet tee shirt effect that she didn't seem to notice or mind. No sign of a brace in the truck, though. In the apartment, they found the photos, misdemeanor pot and pills, and she was a lousy housekeeper, but not much else. No signs of the boyfriend, either.

I instructed the night sergeant to have Tech scan and e-mail Everett Danswaller's photo to Pete and Sarah, then pass the original to Swingin' Dick. I then left a short explanation on his voice mail, forwarding our reality to Atlantic Shores.

Chapter 7
Atlantic Shores

Atlantic Shores is always crowded and comfortable, one of the oldest gay cocktail lounges on the rock. Over the years, the joint has undergone facelifts right along with most of its regular clientele. Lots of flashier, trendier gay clubs and discos have gone up along Duval, but Shores remains the one monument to forbidden love that dates back to when it truly was. Even its nude sunbathing policy has been tolerated, if hardly embraced, by the Disneyphiles in City Hall. Shores keeps our more exotic varietals well away from the camera-toting, free-spending cruise ship crowd as they document the authentic overpriced tourist crawls down at the safe end of Duval.

Shores also remains the one bastion of empire where I can get a proper Manhattan without having to come to blows over it. The bartender knows to carefully spin the correct proportions of bourbon, sweet vermouth and bitters in a stainless-steel ice shaker no more than six rotations, then strain it to exactly fill a highball glass, no ice, no fruit, no stemware.

They idolize Jonah and tolerate me at Shores. True, they have a higher tolerance level than most bars on the rock, but it's not infinite. They seem relieved these days that I'm not as bad as I used to be.

I was into second rounds and second thoughts when Rick arrived, all golden-boy glow.

"I don't like the looks of this one, Jack," he said, wedging in next to me at the claustrophobic bar.

"Swingin'."

He ordered a lite beer and loosened his rep tie shamus style, Joe Friday with an Ivy League signet ring. The thrill of the hunt was all over him like bad aftershave.

"Damn, Jack, after two years, we've finally got a genuine manhunt, the two of us. I've got the head thawing at Fink's Sinks, the lab is running prints, patrols are on the street, e-mails are flying. I've already got this Danswaller's mug in every squad car, bike patrol and marine unit, even the airport. We'll show him how small this island can get."

"You figure he did it, huh?" I said.

"Well, maybe not did-it did it, but he's involved. I mean, he obviously doesn't fit the suspect profile, but he's missing on the day of the murder and he was her contact here. Why? You don't?"

"If he's not dead, we can ask him."

Michaels looked like I'd shot his cat. I ran down the details in the order received, first from Billie's, then from Puss 'n' Boots. He took a sip from his glass, digesting the new information.

"OK, OK, look, try this," he said. "It's Sunday, Danswaller's off, he hitches a ride to Dade, where he steals the Rover. Nice dark windows so she can't make him. This morning, he picks up the guy with the saw, they follow her truck out of Little Havana, waiting for a chance. Or maybe the hitman snatched the Rover, either way. Anyway, she's making deliveries here and there, grabs a Happy Meal in Marathon, stops next to the bridge to picnic, and bingo."

"And the head?"

"OK, there's the double-cross. The killer drops Danswaller off, maybe here, maybe up-island. But before he dumps the Rover, he takes the head to the cold storage, where the temp doesn't know him from Captain Ahab, plants it in the icemaker and he's out of there. Maybe Danswaller doesn't even know he took her head. He drops the Rover and disappears, knowing that when the head is found, we'll come looking for the Bahamian, who planned it all in the first place. Is that island justice or what?"

"Motive?"

Michaels rolled his eyes. "Duh. Did you see her, Jack? She was hot. Maybe she didn't like black guys. Maybe she didn't like guys, period. Whatever. Danswaller can't get in her pants, with her teasing him like that, he gets a head on him, sees blood, fade to credits. How's that for motive?"

"Plausible for now."

"But you don't buy it."

I lit a cigarette.

"I had an epiphany outside Sloppy's tonight," I said. "Looked up and saw suspects all around me."

"Yeah, I thought of that. We're looking for Ernest fucking Hemingway."

"It was so obvious it nearly went right past me. That's right, we're looking for Papa, at the exact moment when there must be a hundred of him down here, fishing and drinking and telling tales. Only one of them is doing more. One of them is killing. You grow up here like I did, you can't help but have a little voodoo in you. I saw the terror on Althea Danswaller's face tonight. It wasn't logical, you know? She was feeling the same gris-gris I'm feeling right now."

"Let's say you're right, Jack, and our Bahamian is toast. What's the motive there?" Michaels asked.

I collected most of the salient points. "Do the girl, with or without a Skil saw, you got to think ex-boyfriend or twist-o. Maybe Danswaller is a spurned lover or a twist-o. I doubt it, but like you say, let's find out. Now, do her and her drop man, it changes everything. Suddenly, you've got the two of them into something—drugs, guns, money laundering. Something. So you look for the connectors. We've got two so far: the magazine outfit and the club."

Jonah emerged from the animated crowd and was surprised to find Michaels beside me. The young detective had a thing for Jonah, as did a hundred other eager young men on the island. I'd tried my best, but no amount of mediation on my part had been able to squelch it. Jonah, of course, was used to the adulation that accompanies minor celebrityhood and had chased many a young man from his dressing room. I think he had been less direct with Rick in deference to my professional relationship with him, a begrudging mentor thing that Jonah considered charming. It was all very squirrelly when our paths crossed in the clubs.

Jonah leaned close to my ear.

"Jack, I've got a couple sisters outside who can't wait to meet you."

Chapter 8
The Sisters

Sometimes it helps to have a woman by your side, even if she is a man. Jonah made up in social graces for my complete lack of them. Sometimes when negotiations would break down and I was about to receive a sidewalk sundae from this bar or that, the angry management treated me far better because I had this remarkably beautiful semblance of a woman at my side. Jonah and I were blood brothers, although the blood so far had been entirely mine.

I welcomed his feminine presence as we joined the sisters seaside on the wooden deck overlooking the Atlantic amid naked ladies enjoying a moonlight swim in the Shores pool.

From the moment I met Jen and Abby Wilde, I knew they were rich, spoiled and scared. Jen, the elder, was toned, tanned and athletic, with a muscular upper body, short, spiky platinum hair and a fairly open dislike for me. Abby was slightly taller, medium build and unkempt in a bookish way, with straight mousy hair and a serious case of the blues.

"Seen Everett Danswaller lately?" I opened. Jonah winced. That courtesy thing, I guess.

"I was about to ask you the same question, detective," Jen said. "It's why you paid the club a visit this evening, isn't it?"

She drew a smoke and slid her pack of imports across the table to me.

"Not exactly," I said.

I tamped one out of the pack and lit it. The smoke had a bite.

"French?"

"Ceylonese, actually. Althea is very concerned. So are we. We saw Everett just last weekend. There was no indication anything was wrong."

Jonah glanced at me. I nodded stay, just chatting here.

"I came by looking for the two of you."

"Then this is about Marty?" Abby said. "Althea said you were asking."

"OK, let's start there. Tell me about Marty Orleans."

The sisters seemed to suddenly trade demeanors. Abby leaned forward in her patio chair, suddenly intense and interested, while Jen sank back, her hooded eyes following naked women around the pool.

"She's in some kind of trouble, isn't she?" Abby asked.

"From the beginning." I smoked and waited.

"Ev, Everett, brought her by the club, near the end of season. He said he met her at the warehouse where he works. She was the new delivery driver. She dressed kind of different, denim skirt, cowboy boots. We had a few drinks, talked some, danced a little. Ev seemed to like her."

She glanced uneasily at her sister. Jen gave her an annoyed look.

"Which is my sister's way of saying we all 'liked her', OK?" she said, gesturing. "And she 'liked' us. Abby. Me. Everett, too, for all I know."

"You went to a few open-mikes at Billie's together," I nudged on.

"She is something very special when she's on stage," Abby assured me. "We were going to make a night of it last night, first Billie's, then some clubs, but we never heard from her. We tried the Travelodge but she wasn't registered. Then we called Ev, but we couldn't get him, either."

I smoked and considered each sister in turn.

"What if I told you they were both missing?"

Abby's mouth dropped and her head snapped toward her big sister. Jen exhaled smoke, disgusted.

"I'd say she found a better deal and took him with her," she said.

"She never would!" Abby's pale face turned bright red.

"Yeah, right," Jen spat. "You might as well know, we were going to back her for her shot at a record deal in Nashville. Or I should say Abby was. Marty and I, we had a little disagreement."

Abby glared at her.

"You were a three-way?" I felt Jonah cringe.

Jen gazed off at the pool, disgusted.

"Abby here seems to think Marty never made it with your buddy Everett. You disagree?" I asked.

The older sister shook her electric-white head. "A man was making her. It's not hard to tell, you know."

"She wasn't that way!" Abby protested.

"She wasn't just *your* way, Abby."

"Let's talk about the club," I detoured. "Why close shop?"

Jen looked away.

"We needed a break," Abby said. "We own the building, so why not? Scene's pretty dead in summer. Travel, relax. You know."

"And have you done any traveling?" I asked.

"Not yet."

"Mmm. So you've just been enjoying the summer. Doing some photography?" I felt Jonah squirm again.

Abby looked at Jen. The big sister fielded it.

"A friend of ours. We let him use the place."

"And this friend's name would be?"

"None of your business, detective. This is about Marty and Ev, remember?"

"Is that why you told your friend Everett to steer clear?"

She shrugged. "We weren't comfortable having Ev in the club when we weren't there, that's all. We're lucky to have help like Ev and Althea. We just don't need them when we're closed. She's with a service, she has other accounts. And he's got a job."

Jonah motioned with his eyes. I turned. Across the pool, Rick was waving his flip phone at me. I stubbed out the fancy cigarette.

"One last question," I glanced at Jonah, "if you don't mind. Puss 'n' Boots. Any relation to PNB Newsstand Services?"

"The initials, I guess. Why?" Jen, cool, back in charge.

Swingin' Dick was still barking into his flip phone when we rejoined him. I fished for a light and filled my lungs with good old domestic stock. Across the terrace, Jen lifted her top over her buzzcut, catching my eye as she emerged from it with a look I couldn't quite read. Was it defiant or seductive? She tossed the top on her chair, then unfastened her bottoms and wedged out of them. I watched through my smoke as she immersed herself in the pool party.

Michaels clicked off, excited.

"Drink up, bud. We've got a floater."

Chapter 9
Floater

The otherworldly fragrance of night-blooming cactus welcomed us as we limboed beneath the crime scene tape and into the courtyard of the Duchess. Rick's officers were arranged around the pool, interviewing witnesses, making notes, trying hard for a homicide scan. The glow from the pool lights cast a festive turquoise hue on the tropical foliage. Lose the body beneath the black tarp, add a few tiki torches, it would have made a nice setting for a drunken wedding reception.

A detective ran it down for us. John Moony, single white male, mid-30s, Ohio driver's license. According to the landlord, Moony arrived in March, rented by the week until May, then went by the month after that. Kept to himself, not a mingler. He may have worked nights; the landlord wasn't sure, didn't think so. Nobody saw him go in or under. No surprise, this late. The pool closed at ten.

I held the tarp up for Swingin' Dick.

"This a nudie house?" he asked his man.

"Optional's what I got. A couple people we talked to weren't shy."

Nude lounging within the confines of secluded guesthouses was tacitly accepted on the rock as a powerful draw for the gay and lesbian tourist trade.

"This guy straight?" Rick continued, scribbling his own notes.

The detective seemed a little flustered with that one, coming from Rick. "They don't know exactly. He was seen with men and women at different times. No one seems to know him."

"Or they don't now," I suggested.

"Drugs?" Rick asked.

"Place is clean. A few 'script poppers'."

Two of Rick's guys looked questioningly at us. I lit a smoke and shrugged. Rick nodded. They gathered up the short, fat man and lugged him to the crime van.

We entered the floater's room. Garden-variety crash pad. Bike, swim mask and fins, towels, camera, beer bottles, letters from home, all distributed haphazardly across on the bed, nightstands, mini-fridge, bathroom counter and closets. Looked like the place had been tossed already, even though the lab guys hadn't gotten there yet. Just the way the guy was. A mess.

A couple uniform cops were busy bagging and tagging. Rick commandeered the wallet while I searched the small clothes closet. A few tropical shirts, some Northern clothes, a couple ball caps, empty luggage. The dresser was more help. I flipped on a portable music player and the local country station came up. A few country tapes were scattered around the place. The top drawer took me further into John Moony's life: a three-pack of condoms, a prescription container with a handful of amyl poppers, extra-large jockeys, several plastic containers of film. Drawer number two contained tee shirts, mostly from bars along the Eastern seaboard, even the newest Hemingway Days issue. Drawer number three held assorted walking shorts, swim trunks, camera paraphernalia and what looked like a white wig. I picked it up. It came apart in two pieces, a rug and beard.

"Check these out, Jack," Michaels said, tossing me an evidence bag.

Inside were several photos of what looked like Moony in full Hemingway attire, surrounded by other Papa look-alikes. The guy had the bulk for the part, no question. The background was too dark to make out the location, but the bearded men were clearly tipping one for old Ern. I checked for a date stamp on the back. They'd been processed earlier that day at a one-hour shop.

"You thinking what I'm thinking?" he asked.

I handed him back the photos.

"You think he took the contest a little too seriously, too?"

"Christ, Jack, I know you've had a few, but focus. This guy does match the killer's description, right?"

"We've already agreed that's not exactly an exclusive club right now."

"OK, but don't you think there just might be a connection? I mean, the girl gets killed, then this guy turns up dead. Just a coincidence?"

"Maybe not. But if he's the killer, why is he dead?"

"The Bahamian, bud. Remember the double-cross? The Bahamian figured the killer was going to set him up, so he came looking for him."

I scattered the puzzle pieces out in my mind and rearranged them over and over as I drove to the morgue. Maybe it was the Manhattans, but I just couldn't get them to fit together as nice and tight as Swingin' Dick.

Ed Fink was seated at the middle table, face to face with the former Marty Orleans. I paused to light up.

"You again? Where's the kid?" The floater was technically Rick's case.

"Still poolside. You made her talk yet?" The place smelled worse than usual. I put that on her head.

"Funny. But I'm glad you stopped by. I want to show you something."

He motioned to a wheeled steel chair with a curved chrome bar for a back rest. I sat next to him, a situation we would both rather do without.

"It's always interesting to see what extreme temperatures do to human tissues."

My eyelids drooped the way they used to in science class.

"The brain won't be completely thawed until morning, but this hematoma here above the ear indicates she did indeed suffer a blow to the head sufficient to render her unconscious. When I get a look inside, I'll be able to confirm whether she was unconscious before the head was removed, for what it's worth."

Her eyes still stared up at me, incredulous. I could hear the sweet voice of my next cocktail calling my name.

He tilted her cold, dripping head, holding it like poor Yorick.

"Of course, as I sat here waiting for your floater to arrive, I examined what I could, kid at Christmas, you know." He pried open the mouth. There was a nauseating wet sound and a trace of light at the back of the throat. "And I found this." Fink turned the face toward the ceiling and inserted a stainless steel probe far up into the neck. He withdrew a mix of red and white mucous.

"We have to do this more often," I said.

"I've already done a slide to confirm that it's semen."

"Uh-huh. Which means we've got oral."

He gave me his best suffer-the-little-children look over his half-lenses.

"Jack, would I get your hopes up for a mere oral? This semen, in considerable quantity I might add, comes from the middle sinus, an area not easily accessible through either the mouth or the nose."

He worked her jaw to illustrate. I didn't like where we were heading.

"Meaning what, exactly?"

"What do you think?" He inserted the probe again and lifted his eyebrows.

"He did the head?"

"That would be my guess."

The Tallahassee twins were precisely where they said they would be, delicately dispatching barflies with the bug-zapper finesse of true Southern women. They opened their arms to welcome me and we picked up where we'd left off the night before, when it was just getting good.

Chapter 10
Nash

Eat too many meals alone, you come to prefer it. By the time you realize you prefer it, you're lost.

Around daybreak, I begged off breakfast with my two far-from-identical young friends and made my way back home to find Nash nestled in my hammock, enjoying the morning sun. It occurred to me that I had never seen her out of uniform, much less in capri pants and a sports bra. She looked island-brown and lovely swaying there in the cotton webbing.

"Loo. This is a pleasant surprise," I said, unlocking the place.

"I took a chance. You'll find a couple messages from me on your machine."

She followed me inside. I threw the blinds and slid open the glass door, welcoming the tangy morning into the *Jackie Oh!* Nash beat me to the coffeepot. My routines, like my cupboards, were both dismal and predictable. She knew where everything was, including my head.

"Our manhunt made the cover of the *Citizen* this morning," Nash said.

"You know Swingin' Dick."

Sarah always gave a little chuckle like a songbird when I called him that.

"And a floater, too," she said over a bare shoulder. "Busy night."

"He thinks they're connected. Thinks the floater did the girl for Danswaller and was going to frame the Bahamian with the ice sculpture. Danswaller gets wind of it and does the floater first."

"Just like that," she said. Skeptical, like me.

"What did the paper have?"

"Papa's boy is lead suspect in girl's murder. Something like that. No names, at least we've still got that."

"They get you?" My answer machine light seemed to be sending Morse code.

She shook her hair. "Pete." I liked it loose.

"And?"

"He confirmed the body was found, but no details pending investigation, so on and so forth. At least, Rick had the good sense to keep the damn cause of death out of it. But Chief's catching no end of shit from the Hemingway Days people already."

"Yeah. I'll have a flamer from Lorian on there, too."

"Anyway, I thought I'd poke around on my day off, follow some hunches. Cool with you?"

"Cool with me, but watch out for the boy wonder."

She brought me a cup of joe and took hers to the wicker poobah chair, sitting sideways, one leg tucked under her.

"Not like the game, is it?" She meant Metro-Dade.

"I don't think about it much." She knew why.

"I think about it," she said, sipping.

"You miss it?"

"Mmm. Sometimes. The squad room. But it was too crazy, wasn't it, Jack?"

"Yeah."

I felt some of the freshness start to escape from the morning.

"You look good like that," I said.

"Like what?" she laughed, feisty, better again.

"Casual. Island girl."

"Thanks, Jack." She considered me a moment, then smiled. "You look, uh…"

"I know. There were these twins, see."

"I don't want to hear about it, thank you."

Cops were good that way. Lots of space.

I offered my pack. She took a cigarette. We lit off my match.

"How did you meet, M. and you? Tell me if it's none of my damn business."

I squinted in the smoky sunlight and told her.

Beginnings. I was working Vice out of Beach, my last assignment before ascending to the game. I drew SoBe. Something about my grooming, I guess; my clothes, my physical appearance, something must have fit the boy-toy thing better than most. I don't know, maybe growing up where I did, I understood the rituals of the gay world a little better. Whatever, South Beach welcomed me. I began to feel first a belonging, and then an identity, almost instantly.

The deeper I allowed myself to sink into the human carnival that was SoBe, the more effective I became at acquiring information and tracing leads. But undercover, success becomes a double-edged sword. If you're too good at it, your fellow officers become suspicious or resentful.

Pretty soon they're feeding the rumor mill. Then it's just a matter of time before the suits start wondering if you're using.

We were working a sting setup on a Jamaican posse. My job was to feed cash to a little blowfish, buying my way in. Further up the food chain, well above my radar, M. was deep undercover with the feds, playing a trust fund wild child with an insatiable gold-dust habit. Wires got crossed downtown. When the deal went south, M. and I finally met, at gunpoint, in the Fontainebleau Hotel on Miami Beach, tired, wired, and hung out to dry. We often wondered what would have happened if the Jamaicans had not played it out the way they did.

"That night we thought we were toasting our careers goodbye," I said. "That was the start of it."

"The way you tell it, it almost sounds romantic."

"Loo, you had to be there. We had no idea until we were barrel to barrel."

To finish the tale, I emerged from my year undercover labeled a coke fag by the rumor mill. Word from on high was that my shot at a Homicide ticket was over. That's when Pete stepped in. He drew the deep water even then and he got me in the game. Pete became Homicide chief a short time later and I became his star performer. With M. in my life, everything was golden.

But golden doesn't last. Two years ago, it all blew up. A few entrepreneurs in Narco were caught opening their own 401Ks with seized drug money, throwing Metro-Dade into yet another IAD purge. Internal Affairs had never looked crosswise at me, even with the rumors, but after a while it hardly mattered, everyone was presumed dirty. The paranoia and recrimination became so bad you couldn't trust your own backup. The choice was simple: stay and risk eventual indictment—because of what you saw or did not see, heard or did not hear, who you stood up for or to—or update the old resume.

A lot of the older guys around Metro dream of stepping off to the relative calm of Monroe Country. To them, the Keys is the Promised Land: big, wild and wacky enough to keep them young, yet small, quiet and sparse enough to allow for an actual family life, maybe even some fishing. Ironically, Metro-Dade was busy luring Monroe County sheriffs up to the game to fill the shoes of the bad seeds IAD was shipping off to Raiford.

I didn't figure Pete to be looking at the Keys. He could go anywhere with his experience. But six months later, shortly after I lost M., Pete signed on as chief at Monroe Country. Major bombshell. And shortly after that he pulled me from my burning life.

I washed ashore in Key Weird. I was a real mess that first year back, incorrigible, belligerent, irresponsible, occasionally brilliant, frequently worthless. Or so I'm told. If I've shown any progress since, it's been mostly due to the creatures of the night. They fished me half-dead from an alcohol grave, gave me warmth when I didn't know I was cold, comforted me, and made me feel that, if nothing else, it would be utterly gauche to depart this world so soon. They'd seen too many pretty corpses these days, I guess. And Jonah always assured me that all things are possible, even saving my sorry hide. And he should know; he had his choice of restrooms.

We sat in silence, Loo and me, watching the shorebirds feast, each of us lost in our own memories of the game.

"Seems like you'll never stop hurting, huh?" Nash said.

I mashed my cigarette in the ashtray.

"I should crash." Like that could happen, or would be any solution if it did.

"I'm down for the day," Nash said, depositing her mug in the galley. "Check you later, Jack."

I watched as she climbed the ramp to her sports car.

Check you later, Jack.

I tried whispering it to myself.

Chapter 11
German Gossip

I woke up with a beauty and wondered if I was getting too old for tequila. I enjoyed the ritual of it, sure, and never more so than when flanked by two sun-kissed Southern blondes with very specific appetites. But as an intoxicant, the stuff was too scatter-shot, too insincere, too generalized for my purpose. Tequila would never get me where I hoped Manhattans would, i.e. off the planet.

Rain had fallen. That's when I realized I must have actually slept or passed out, one. Nash and the morning started coming back to me. I nuked a cup of the coffee she'd made hours ago.

I'd never talked about M. with Nash before. Most anyone who knows me stays well away from the subject. Even with Pete, the few times, we talked around it, the way men will. With Jonah, I poured my soul out in a drunken spew a time or two, but he mostly listens, which I take to mean he knows how useless it is. With Nash, I don't know. It was more than cop to cop. She knew the official version. Everybody did. But I got the feeling she knew there was more to it. Like I say, she's sharp.

I threw on a pair of gym shorts and walked my coffee outside. The deck of the *Jackie Oh!* was wet and cool. I settled into the hammock. The passing thunderheads were drifting off into the Atlantic.

Jurgen, the dark one, was hosing down the *Popinjay* next door. There were no secrets with these Speedo guys; I could pick his rigging out in a blind lineup. I saluted him with my coffee mug. He shut down the spray.

"Jack, did we see you at Shores last night?"

"Mmm."

"We spoke with Jonah."

"Sure." Who didn't?

He sat down on his clean wet upper deck, his enormous arms perched between the rails. "You have some interest in Club Puss 'n' Boots?"

"Maybe. Why?"

Jurgen glanced toward the street.

"Horst and I have heard things, that's all."

I nodded, continue.

"Because they are closed, you see. They did not close before. The sisters who own it, they couldn't agree on that. It has never been closed in summer before. Something changed their minds, I think."

The slightest constriction of Key Weird nightlife was always a matter of some concern to them.

"You know the sisters?"

"Yes, sure. The pretty one's Jen, short for Genevieve. She is the one who didn't want to close. She likes the nightlife. But the other one, Abby, she doesn't join the party. She's the little bookkeeper. It was her idea, I think."

"So they save a few bucks. What's wrong with that?"

"Well, it all started when the little cowgirl came to town."

"Mmm. The little cowgirl would be?" The name of the murdered girl wasn't public knowledge yet.

"Her name is Marty. I don't know if that's her real name. Later, they called her Marty Party. We were there one night…oh, I shouldn't."

My interested expression egged him on.

"She was very wild with the dancing. Do you know her?"

"Mmm," I nodded.

"Do you know the owner, Jen?"

I nodded again. I was beginning to.

"Well, everybody thought Jen and Marty Party were lovers. Who knows, right? But that night you could tell things were different in the club. More electric, you know how it gets. Anyway, Jen and Marty seemed to be challenging each other dancing, to see who could be the most outrageous. Things got hotter and hotter until they were both topless. Several others, too. One thing led to another and pretty soon Marty Party was dancing with nothing on but her cowboy boots. Nothing. Dancing with everyone, dancing with herself. Someone lifted her up on a table and she was wiggling and shaking, touching herself, everybody touching her, men and women. Anyway, when Marty Party did that, you could tell Jen was angry behind her party smile. Then Marty brought the schwartzer up there with her, the black guy everybody calls Slim, and started undressing him. Well, Marty got his hat and shirt off and was going for his candy, everybody cheering her on, when Jen suddenly stopped the music. She just stood there at the

DJ booth, glaring at Marty Party and Slim. Those two grabbed the clothes they could find and left. The music started back again, but that cooled things off very fast."

"Cigarette?" I teased him. If he got it, he never let on.

"A few days later, we went back. That's when we found out they were closed for summer."

I pictured Jen as I had seen her by moonlight, her lean, muscular body sheathed in an all-over tan, clean shaven and glowing like marble.

"Have you seen them out clubbing since they closed?"

"Yes. Not like that, of course. But we did see Jen recently at the Poinciana Lounge, with Marty Party as a matter of fact. I guess it must have been the little cowgirl's idea."

"You and Horst, at the Point?" Key Weird's only country line-dance venue.

Jurgen rolled his eyes.

"He's on some kind of Western kick, I guess. Tight asses and boots, I can understand, but oh Jack, that music…" He made the universal face of disgust.

I laughed and pried myself out of the hammock.

"Thanks. Interesting stuff."

He rose above my sightline, then knelt down.

"Jack, if there's any chance they'll reconsider, please ask them to open Puss 'n' Boots. I don't think I'm a honky-tonk angel."

I checked e-mail before hitting the shower. The truck report was in. The lab rats found victim-only prints in the cargo area. On the doors and in part of the cab, including the radio dials, they'd come up with 'cleans', essentially bald prints left behind when some form of Latex glove or fast-dry liquid coating had been used to cover up the identifying whorls. A second lab report from the KWPD rats found numerous prints on the block-ice machine predictably matching those of Everett Danswaller, who'd been logged several years prior on a failure-to-appear warrant. No 'cleans' were found, however.

While the reports printed out, I dialed Fink. Nearing five, he'd be locking up.

"Monroe County Coroner."

"What happened with the floater?"

"Well, in a nutshell, Jack, he wasn't."

"Wasn't what?"

"A floater. Our Mr. Moony died a far different, and drier, death, I'm afraid. What were we taught to never, never mix with water, Jack? Remember?"

"Bourbon?"

"Electricity, Jack, electricity. I'm afraid Mr. Moony took a rather serious helping of it, completed a circuit in some way, and it stopped his heart. The blood tests confirm the myocardial infarction, but from what I can tell of the brain functions, Mr. Moony's neural system would have been incapable of supporting life had he survived it. Dead in the water, yes. Dead *from* the water, no."

"Which rules out suicide."

"I think we have to, yes. Unless you can suggest how a 34-year-old male with no brain and respiratory functions could walk across a courtyard for a midnight swim."

"When did you know, Eddie? I mean, that he wasn't a floater."

"I don't know. Ten, fifteen minutes after you left, they brought him in. You just know, with floaters. The color.

Plus, they usually blow up subdurally like a water balloon. As soon as I cut into the pleural cavity and didn't hit a gusher, it was pretty obvious."

"Tox?"

"The guy was a garbage disposal. Little of this, a little of that. Mostly THC and uppers, but we've got traces of coke, meth, even a little horse powder in him. And alcohol, of course. Call the kid. He's got this one all figured out."

"Yeah, I know. What about the head?"

"Jack, you're familiar with the garrote?"

"I'm not much of a tool guy, Eddie."

"It's a strong thin cord or wire with handles, used for strangulation."

"Sounds handy."

"It's very effective on its own merits. In this case, however, the killer added a twist to the ancient weapon. Tiny serrations, no larger than the teeth of your average hacksaw. When combined with the high tensile strength and flexibility of a garrote, a skilled user can whip-saw through human tissue and bone with little effort. Although if time were a factor, a good circular saw would have been the way to go. Messier, but faster. If you had the room, a ban saw would also be a good choice."

"Thanks, Eddie."

"I'll see you Friday, Jack. I've got a date with the biggest billfish in Papa's tournament at sunrise tomorrow. Try and keep the body count down until I get back."

Chapter 12
The Point

Loo joined me at the Point shortly after eight. Line-dance lessons had just concluded, but eager students were still out on the floor busting moves to the house system. You couldn't actually look out of place at the Point, especially in summer, but you sure could feel it. We huddled at a bar table well off to the side.

"I spoke with Althea Danswaller today," Nash said, helping herself to a smoke from my pack. "She's worried sick, what with the story in the paper and on TV now."

"Think she's heard from him?"

"Hard to say. She damn sure wouldn't tell me if she had. She's ready to fight for him if she has to. One look around their place, it's no wonder."

"Poor, huh?"

"Just the opposite. She's living better than I am, from the looks of it. I was expecting barefoot kids and chickens on the couch, but that's not them. He must be doing all right, because what I saw you can't buy on a cleaning-woman's wages."

"Anything on the sisters?"

"She wasn't sharing much. I gather the younger one runs the business, cuts the checks and works with the vendors. Althea was cool with her. The older one is more or less the hostess and front of the house. She didn't have anything good to say about her. I sensed there may have been something between this Jen and the brother, but Althea didn't come right out and tell me. I get the impression she thinks the older sister got him into some fast living he didn't know how to get out of."

"She may be right." I related my conversation with the *Popinjay* muscle boy.

"So that's what brings us here." She seemed relieved that it hadn't been my idea.

"It makes sense. If the sisters were taking a chance to help launch Marty Orleans, they might have been thinking of polishing her act in here."

An enormous man in an impossible-size Poinciana Lounge tee shirt and triple-X jeans approached us, wiping his hands on a bar towel. His long gray hair was pulled back in a ponytail and his enormous moustache didn't quite cover a couple gold teeth up front.

"I'm Mountain. You two wanted to see me?" His voice sounded like a dump truck unloading gravel.

We took turns wringing the manager's damp hand.

"We're looking for information on a woman named Marty Orleans. Ring a bell?"

"Sure, I know Marty. Sits in with the house band now and then. You're not going to tell me she's under-age?"

"Would you believe it if I did?"

"Hell no, but who can tell, these kids anymore? If we didn't card her…"

"It's nothing like that. She's legal. We're interested in anything you might know about her. Who she hangs with, that sort of thing."

He rubbed his huge face in thought.

"Let's see. She first started coming in a few months back with a black dude. Skip, Slim, something like that. He wasn't any problem but I don't think he liked the place much. Lately I seen her with a couple dykes. Even danced with them, which was kinda funny 'cause I didn't think she was that way. Surprised the band, too. They got on real good with her, considering she doesn't live down here. But hell, a country boy will try anyway. She also hung out with the Moonman, guy named Moony. He's a photographer. At least that's what he tells the ladies."

"What do you know about him?"

"Moony? He's a regular. Probably be in tonight. Short, stocky guy. He can be a party animal, but keeps to himself mostly. I think he does a little loco weed out back with the band sometimes, but he's no trouble."

"Have you seen him in his Hemingway outfit?" Nash wondered.

Mountain laughed. It looked like a gold rush and sounded like a landslide.

"Oh man, were you here? Those dudes held a special happy hour shindig here Saturday night to kick off their week. I didn't know he was into that, but I'll be damned if he didn't make a pretty good one himself. He took pictures that night, too. He's going to bring them by so we can put them up on our board."

"Does he do any serious photography that you know of?" Loo asked.

"Depends what you mean by serious. He's always carrying that fancy camera with him. Shoots pictures of the band sometimes. Tell you the truth, I think he just uses it to get chicks. He ain't holdin' a strong hand in the looks department, but maybe he convinces them they can be models or something, you know? Break into show business."

"Is that how he met Marty Orleans?" I asked.

"Wouldn't surprise me. She's going to be a star or die trying, that one. If anyone can out-hustle a hustler, she can. Maybe he took some pictures of her on stage and she wants to use them for promotion or something. Who knows what goes on in people's heads, right?"

"Who knows," I agreed. "One last question. Did you get the feeling there was anything physical between Moony and Marty Orleans?"

"You know Moony?" he asked.

I shook my head no.

"He should be so lucky."

The band drove us out of there. I walked Loo to her tiny convertible, blowing fresh smoke into the clear, humid evening as the music bounced around the parking lot.

"Looks like Moony's in the mix, all right," I said. "I'm just not sure how."

"Unfortunately, Rick is," she reminded me.

I borrowed her cell phone and left the high points of our interview with Mountain on Swingin' Dick's machine.

Nash fished her keys out of her shoulder-bag. Her brow had a way of setting itself when she was deep in thought and it was set that way now. She gathered her long windswept hair into a bouquet of curls and tied it back for the ride up-island.

"Maybe finding Slim will change his mind, one way or another," I said, handing her the flip phone.

"Never say never. Me, I'm going to take a look at some bank records, first thing. The Danswallers don't add up. Neither do these two. Sounds like they were either hustling each other or partners in something and it got them killed."

I hated records searches. No patience for it. I offered her my pack. She shook her head. She still had that thinking look. I pulled a smoke and slipped it behind her ear.

"One for the road, JIC."

Jonah had just wrapped the early set at Club Chameleon when I arrived. The place was already exceeding the fragrance limit. When things get smoky, as they always do, it's even worse, like being forcibly wrestled into the bosom of your chain-smoking great-aunt.

I'd been working with the young Oriental bartender on the proper construction of a Manhattan, but there was so much general pandemonium surrounding him most nights that his pours invariably fell long or short of the mark. At least, he remembered to leave the cherry out.

Jonah was clad in his usual between-set attire, plush full-length orchid-colored Saks terry robe and lime green aqua booties. Two backdoor Johnnies gave me the look as Jonah graciously shooed them on their way and closed the door behind us. I placed my Manhattan on the antique silver butler and fell into my chair, the wingback.

"So it turns out this floater last night? He's connected. Knows her through the Point. Country fan. Plus, he's a photographer. Lab's souping his film now."

Jonah popped a fresh mineral water.

"Have you found anyone who has not slept with this tramp?"

"You and me, and I'm not so sure about me. Plus, the killer's sicker than we thought. Turns out he did her head."

"*Did* her head?"

I nodded. "After."

"Oh please!"

"So I've got this twist-o running around sawing off heads and frying fat guys and approximately half the island fits his description right now. I've got Swingin' Dick out there telling the press the fat guy did her for Danswaller. I've got the missing Bahamian who's either behind both murders or next in line. And I've got the twisted sisters who know more than they're telling. How'd your set go?"

"Lovely, thank you."

"Nash was down today. She's jumping on bank accounts tomorrow. Turns out Danswaller's living large and there may be business between the fat boy and our headless lady."

"Don't these things always come down to money?"

"Mmm."

"How were the twins, by the way?" Jonah's sources were both faster and more reliable than mine. He would have made a pretty good dick, except for the wardrobe.

"I swear, they're the reason God made tourists. I still hurt."

He nudged his wig off its clear plastic head and cradled the orb in his lap, running his fingers over it. "But you're thinking about someone else. I see a very pretty woman.

Strong, athletic, short blonde hair…” Jonah prided himself on his fine-honed sense for romantic chemistry.

I took a sip and shook him off.

“You know the rules: Don’t bother with the local girls.”

He just smiled. I rolled my eyes.

“Jonah, she’s a lesbian. Les-bi-an.”

“Maybe, maybe not. But she’s also here.”

Chapter 13
Jen

I would be proven wrong in a big way about Jen, of course. Under normal circumstances, I would have recognized instantly the look she gave me across a crowded pool. But these were far from normal circumstances, even by Key Weird standards. And she was, if not exactly a suspect, at least one of the keys to the puzzle.

Was I surprised to find her at the Chameleon that night, sitting at a deuce in the rear, looking like a frat-boy's dream? Maybe. But it's a small island; when two forces attract, there's really so little to get in their way. I've seen longshots that would have fallen off anyone's tote board come in on this rock, for good or ill. This is no place to bet against dancing penguins.

"We meet again," I said in greeting.

"Under better circumstances, I hope," she demurred.

I flagged Chan to build me one as Jen invited me to join her.

I lit her crazy brand and one of my own. She smiled self-consciously and glanced away as I studied her in the candlelight.

"We didn't have a chance to discuss our mutual friend last night," she said. "How did you and Jonah meet?"

My turn to smile. "The first time, or recently?"

"The first time, then."

"That would be behind the shop building at the high school one Friday night. It was football season. We had this mean bunch. Every class does. They caught Jonah and another guy from the drama club back there smoking pot before a game and decided to teach the fags a lesson. I was a jock. Track and basketball mostly. We were just hanging out before the game when we heard the fight. Broke it up before anybody looked too bad. After that, I knew Jonah to say hi to in the halls, but we weren't in the same crowd."

"And recently?" She was studying me a little, too.

"Recently, I guess you could say he's returned the favor many times over." She waited for more, but I didn't really want to go into it.

"So, when did you come back?"

"Coming up on two years now. Can't believe it myself sometimes. I wandered into this club in no condition to behave. Jonah recognized me and helped me out."

"You seem to fit in well. For a cop."

"Thanks, I think."

"Tell me, do cops dance?"

"Yes, but not well."

I showed her, for several songs. There was a time I could dance, a time when I worked at it for the Vice job, even a time when I enjoyed it. All before I lost M. Now I tend to be that trouble guy in the corner the bouncer keeps one eye on. Jen, on the other hand, was in her element out there. Although we probably logged, hour for hour, roughly the same amount of time in bars, hers involved moving her body to the beat, whether at work or at play, and it showed, believe me. The way she seemed to collect the rhythm inside her and then serve it to me mixed with her own was off the meter. The pleasure in her eyes, the high heat of her body, the flush to her cheeks and the quick breaths through those full, parted lips, all these things portended a marvelous, memorable roll in the sheets in some bright frat-boy future.

"Not bad. For a cop." She lit us both.

"You're being kind."

She laughed, giggled almost, the most relaxed I'd seen her.

"What?"

"You're not gay!"

I shrugged. "It's a free country."

"I had my doubts, Jack. Honest."

"Is that what this is about? To see?"

"Cool down. Jonah points you out to me at Shores, you're drinking with Ricky, what am I supposed to think?"

"You know Michaels?"

"Sure. Everybody knows Ricky."

I brooded. She almost-giggled, controlled but they were there.

She leaned over suddenly and kissed me, long and hard.

"I bet you were wondering, too," she whispered.

Like that was past tense.

"How do *you* know Jonah? You haven't said."

"Everyone knows Jonah, don't they? I met him when we first came down. Abby had grander ideas then, about doing a cabaret. Jonah talked some sense into us. He probably doesn't even remember. We were backstage, like everybody else."

"Puss 'n' Boots seems to be doing well," I said.

"Are you working now, Jack?"

"No, just observing."

"The club's been a lot of work. You don't just open your doors in this town and expect miracles. There are plenty of cheeks to kiss. Asses, too."

The emcee gave Jonah an appropriately risqué introduction. Jen turned her chair next to mine, placed her hand on my thigh and we fell back and watched his set. I'd seen it countless times and was never disappointed. I could relax knowing I would be completely overlooked in his funny, endearing give-and-take with the audience. It was understood. He occasionally sent particular lines of song my way with a teasing glance and did so that night a couple of times, hello young lovers, luck be a lady and so forth.

After the set, we went directly to her place.

The entrance to the stilt house was lush with tropical foliage. I held the wooden gate for her, she tugged me into the small courtyard and we kissed in the humid night air. Then she took my hand and pulled me upstairs. The interior was open and modern, with a vaguely oriental feeling to it, low unstructured furniture, rich dark woods, tatami mats throughout.

I felt a wet nose on my ankle as she closed the door.

"Lucien," she cooed, picking up the wriggling honey-colored handful of Golden Retriever at my feet. He was all puppy teeth and full of the devil.

I held him and petted him, both strange sensations in my arid life. He wanted to play and most anything would do, a cup, a spoon, the cap from a whiskey bottle. He ran out of steam quickly. Jen laid him gently into a padded basket.

The view of the Gulf from the bedroom nearly rivaled the sight of her as she slid out of her slip dress, naked underneath.

We made love the first time without voicing a word. I may have offered whispered monosyllables of thanksgiving after, and may have heard a clenched sigh or two of explicit approval, or they may have been merely echoes from the past. But the second time, unafraid, we shared more of ourselves. In that arena, she was as imaginative and articulate as she was precocious and wanton. After, she smoked, we talked. I poured drinks, we talked. I smoked, she dozed. She woke, I arose. We went on like that through much of the night, learning ever more adventurous ways to please the different people we slowly became to each other. By the time dawn moved in, we had attained a state of sated grace.

Naked and beautiful in the morning sun, she walked me to her gate. There we kissed, finally laughing out loud at how sore even our lips had become.

I got most of the distance to the Jeep when she called out.

"Well, aren't you going to ask me?"

I turned. I'd just fished my JIC from my shirt pocket. It was bent but salvageable. She giggled. I must have been a sight.

"Ask you what?"

"If I'm a lesbian?"

"Mmm." I drew in the smoke. "OK, are you?"

I got a final glimpse of her magnificent tanned behind as she bent to pick up Lucien.

"Just have to see," she teased.

Then the gate swung shut.

Chapter 14
The Risks

Back on the *Jackie Oh!* I found a note from Pete, rather urgently requesting the pleasure of my company at a morning meet with our counterparts on the Key Weird side. I had just enough time to brew some joe and play what's my love life over a shave.

We both knew the risks so well, I suppose it was inevitable that we would ignore them. Still, those early days together with M. seemed anything but dangerous. I had my shiny new Homicide shield, a flat in the Grove and the first normal work schedule I'd ever known. She'd been ceremoniously decorated, in part for not capping me, then reassigned to a drug surveillance unit that placed her home more nights than not. We were in cop heaven, if such a place exists.

In the first days, during what the department euphemistically termed my 'drying out' leave, I was a handful: edgy, spiteful, lost in my own skin. They felt better about 'drying out', calling it that, like I'd downed one too many beers. Those who knew what it was like to come off flake, those who had maybe survived similar lives undercover where the lines between right and wrong had a way of running right up your nose, saw the irony in 'drying out'. I was so dry I crackled. What I needed was wet. What I got was beyond wet, beyond what I could have imagined. What I got was M.

We kept an almost comical distance between us, especially in those first nervous weeks. She knew what I was dealing with and gave me plenty of room to rant and rave at the fires burning just beneath my skin. She would be at my side, running along the jetty in the middle of the night, while I tried to induce sleep. She poured liquids and strength and love into me slowly, without ever giving me more than I could take or coming closer than I could stand. The world of SoBe had been a diet of candy, and like a kid, I was petulant, moody, and at times full-tantrum outraged at suddenly being denied it. My mind was sound and anxious to be whole again. But first, I knew I must kill the fire raging within.

I asked M. to help me and she did. Without being aware of the process, I was suddenly clean, sharp and sober, whole again thanks to M. Not even so much as a beer touched my lips for the remainder of her life. She was a champ.

What we found when the powder finally cleared were a couple peas of a pod, two born cops, united in our love of the game. I know, it never works. We tried to be the exception that proves the rule. It's tough enough when two worlds collide in the mass hallucination that is law enforcement. We had to do it the hard way: hot young dick from arguably the most corrupt metro police force in the country meets the jewel of the almighty fed's southeastern division. Let's just say you didn't have to ask who was who at the Christmas party.

Most cases like ours end long before tragedy, of course. Most just end, one day or the next, not with a bang but a whimper. There's just so little left when the job gets through with you, it doesn't leave much to talk about but shop. And I guess we did our share of that, although it never became the be-all and end-all it is with some. I think when you've been muzzle to muzzle with someone, a hummingbird's cough away from eternity, it maybe changes your choice of topics. We talked about a lot of things over my bad cooking, candlelit baths and holding hands on the beach. What remains in my mind from back then is a lot of laughter. That's the sound I miss the most.

Risks. In a way, they're what lure you to the game in the first place. Cops are not much different from the rail birds up at Hialeah, placing their bets and taking their chances. Maybe we're closer to the jockeys, actually, perched atop something uncontrollable, leaning this way and that, giving at least the illusion that we can somehow affect the outcome.

I had not taken a risk since that overcast December day when I watched M. slowly leave the planet without me.

Not until last night.

Pete always dressed for his trips down-island. Liked to take his Metro-Dade suits for a walk the way some people drive the warranty out of their tires. Plus, he knew it gave him a symbolic edge over Michaelangelo Gianetti, Key West's chief of police. Johnny, short for Gianetti, a no-nonsense spit-and-polish guy from Mean Streets, New Yawk, spent most of his life lugging a hardware store on his person and he wasn't about to kick now. I think it played well with some of them at city hall, having this sinister-looking character in full battle garb striding the halls on their behalf. Seeing little Johnny and Pete together brought to mind the second and third bananas in a prison-break movie, Johnny the human mole, Pete the one you wonder how in Christ he was going to fit through the tunnel.

It was quite a tableau when I arrived, Johnny in his usual little Fuhrer getup, Pete in his banker's costume and Michaels out of jacket, looking like a Hollywood poster dick, his pinpoint oxford rolled at the cuffs, showing off his shoulder holster. Then again, who was I to cast aspersions, having just donated a half-pint in a half-dozen spots, sprucing up just enough to avoid ridicule at the early-morning powwow?

We spread the case out on the table. Pete and Johnny were due before the city-county executive council pronto to explain where we stood, best-guess-scenario wise. Johnny was not what you'd call a deep thinker, in this or any other situation. You knew he'd always cover the political angles long before getting a hair out of place over such high-concept issues as right and wrong or protecting the public. Can't chase the bad guys without a permit, he would say in his own defense. Meaning a badge.

"OK, we each got a stiff here. Jacky says we got connections, between the broad and the smoke, the broad and the floater. Two of the three of them are dead, ergo the third one did it. Favor, say I."

Johnny never liked it when I laughed. Neither did Pete, who after all had to work with the guy.

"What's so funny, Dodge?"

Anyone without hardware had to explain himself, I guess.

"I don't know, it's early for me so maybe I'm off here, but shouldn't we obtain some evidence before we declare open season on Everett Danswaller? Hypothetically, I mean."

It was Swingin' Dick's turn to burn, having shot his mouth off to the press.

"Jack, not every murder is some great convoluted crime of the century, you know. Most of the time they're just simple, stupid human passions run amok. Like this one, the old double-cross gone bad. Why do you want to make more of it? Sometimes things are what they are."

"And sometimes they aren't," I said. "Stop me if you've heard this, but we've got no weapon on either one of them, we've got a pretty wild story that makes circumstantial look good, and we've got a missing player mixed up in all this whose only crime could be that he's scared shitless of us. And judging from what I'm hearing, he's got good reason."

Rick looked away in disgust. Johnny squinted at me like a bouncer who'd just decided he'd had enough. Pete rocked forward in his chair.

"Cool off, everybody," he said, "I think we're all wound a little tight here over nothing. What the council really wants to know is whether they need to pull the plug on Hemingway Days under the circumstances, not who did it. We've already done some speculating in the paper about that and there's no taking it back now anyway. But if we think it's reasonable to assume that John Moony was involved in the girl's death, and at this point I would have to say it is, I think we can consider the connection to the festival closed. I see no reason to stop the party. Johnny?"

"Nah. We got our guy. Besides, the town could use the dough."

Rick got up. He never sat well or for long.

"I've got a warrant coming down on Danswaller," he said, giving me a defiant look. "You can tell them that."

"Tell me it's not murder one." I said.

He nodded.

There I went, laughing again.

The chiefs stood. This was over.

Down the hall, Pete and I detoured to strain some coffee.

"You get to that boy," he said to the tile wall before us.

"Was my head ever that thick?"

Pete laughed.

"You grew up in a hurry, Jack. He's all book-learning, that one."

"I kind of hate to spoil his fun," I admitted.

He grinned.

"Yeah, but you will."

I knew a few of the Key Weird lab rats from clubbing. They were not happy with Johnny's regimen, especially as it related to uniforms and grooming. Unlike our disorderly orderlies, who looked like refugees from a surfer cult when they weren't wrapped for action, Key Weird lab animals were expected to maintain an almost military appearance on the job, even down in the tombs.

Nancy in Photo had just finished printing Moony's rolls and was bagging and tagging them when I joined her under the red lights.

"Jack," she said, giving me a cheek. "I was about to send these up to Ricky Ricardo."

"My lucky day. What've we got?"

"Boys will be boys. Come on."

She led me out of the darkroom and into her weasel-warren cubicle. I'd admired her red hair the few times we'd met on crime scenes, and we shared a closeness that bordered on more, but she wasn't a night owl so there wasn't much to work with there.

"Apparently your Mr. Bubbles liked to watch," she said, handing me the stack.

I rifled through them once for the scan, then studied them closer. There was little left in the way of physical possibilities between two men and a woman that was not documented in the black-and-white prints. Hard core pornography of the posed variety, the kind you can practically hear the shooter barking, "Lift this! Turn that!"

"Tell me about these. From a photographer's point of view." I handed part of the stack to her.

She smiled first, thinking I was kidding, then shrugged and looked them over.

"Well, they're shot on pretty slow stock, which means he used a tripod and lights. He had a setup like a studio, fixed lights and sequenced flash. But look, here he's washing out, and here too, so he hasn't really learned how to balance them yet."

"What about the images?"

"What about them, Jack?" Her oh-come-on grin.

"You know, the angles, how they're set up, that sort of thing."

She wrinkled her nose dubiously but returned to the task.

"Well, obviously the composition is centered on the woman."

Indeed. Throughout the entire stack, as many as a hundred shots, the unabashed Martina Orlovsky was featured front and center, back and center, side and center. Her body was joined at the usual openings, and in various combinations, by two riggings, one black, the other white. Except for the occasional forearm in the frame or a hand atop her head, the males existed as lower torsos only, throughout. No faces, no upper bodies, no legs below mid-thigh.

"He uses screens for backdrop. You can see the bottom of one, just barely in frame, here. Screen sides creep into the frame all over the place, if you look for them."

She rifled through the stack, looking for examples.

"Here's one. Here, he shot above the top of the screen. Look."

"Well, that would be a tough angle," I said.

"Mmm." Which I took as noncommittal, on the shot or the position, I couldn't tell which.

She reached into her desk clutter for a magnifying loupe and held it flush to the print.

"There's a lighted sign of some kind behind it. I can make out an F or…"

"An E."

"Exit sign. Sure."

She looked up.

"More?" she asked.

"Is there more?"

She shuffled through the deck.

"Like I say, his use of lighting is primitive. She's a very pretty woman. You take away the flying dick brothers, he could have made her beautiful, if it meant anything to him. Black-and-white is a good medium for that. But he didn't. I guess what I'm saying is, I don't think he shot them for himself. Not if he felt anything for her."

"See much porn though here, Nance?"

She laughed. "Who needs porn when you've got gore, huh?"

"But you see some."

"Sure. Evidence, like this. And ID cases."

"And this?"

"It's sure amateur enough."

She ran to catch a timer bell. I shuffled through the stack for a couple arm and hand shots I'd noticed. I examined them through her loupe until I was satisfied, then slipped them into my shirt.

I had an unlit cigarette already stuck in my grin as I winked thanks to her on my way out.

Chapter 15
Island Woman

Jen and a couple girlfriends were tanning au natch when I arrived. She extended her cocoa-brown body against me and greeted me with a generous kiss that carried a sweet marijuana aftertaste. Lucien yelped and bit at the weathered laces of my topsiders. It was just after ten; Pete and Johnny would be through the worst of it by now.

"Come on, join us." The corners of her lips curled up in a wicked little smile as she hung from my neck.

"Can't stay."

She slowly lowered off her toes.

"You're working." A chill came into her voice.

I stooped to calm the golden puppy.

"All play and no work," I said, trying for glib. I was hopeful, after all, even with what we had to discuss. Who wouldn't be after last night?

She led me to the kitchen and brought me a beer. I had my choice of seats, a panoramic view of shrimpers farming the blue Atlantic or two attractive females sunning their wrappers on the Gulf side. Tough choice. She tossed on a gauzy peek-a-boo cover-up and perched catlike across from me.

"Jen, let's talk about John Moony."

She stretched for her French cuts and held my hand as I lit one for her.

"I read. What a tragedy, drowning like that."

"I've just seen his work."

She gazed out through her smoke at the shimmering Atlantic, considering the deeper meaning of what I'd just said.

"John really wanted to be someone," she said at last. "He wasn't much of a photographer, I guess, but he made a good living doing what he did."

"How did you meet him?"

"Marty. She brought him by the club. Another stray, trying to fit into her big dreams. She was the one they found, wasn't she? The girl murdered on the bridge?"

When I didn't answer, her eyes lowered. For a split second, a hint of sadness passed through her features like a current, then it was gone.

"Next question: How did you come to let Moony use the club for his shoots?"

She shrugged, squinting out to sea, wistful or bored, one.

"We were closing, Marty asked, we said sure, why not?"

"Did you know what they were shooting?"

"Well, I assumed it wasn't waxed fruit. Look, Jack, Marty is...*was* a wild child. In fact, you probably would have liked her. A lot. Men did. She wasn't shy about things. She used to say she was riding a rocket to the stars. She was fun in bed, great in bed, but you didn't think you could own her, you know? Any more than you could own a tropical storm or a good hard fuck. She was a hustler, Jack. She worked hard to get places and meet people who could help her. She thought John might be one of those people, and who knows? Stranger things have happened."

"And your buddy Everett was helping out?"

She got that annoyed look I'd seen the other night. It seemed to come on when discussion turned to humans who made less-than-intelligent choices with their lives. Her voice turned dull and monotone, like a child reciting poetry against her will.

"I take some of the blame for Everett. He was such a good worker around the place, moving furniture, helping out decorating when we needed him. As a reward, I'd buy him a drink now and then, let him hang out a little, that's all. Then he brought Marty around and all that changed. He became sort of like her entourage, driving her here, driving her back to the motel, since all she had was that huge truck. She bought him this black cowboy hat and pretty soon everyone was calling him Slim, like he was one of our customers, not our handyman. When she brought Moony around, at first we thought it was a good sign, you know, like she'd gotten tired of Slim and he could go back to being Everett instead of Superfly. But then he and Moony became tight. Don't ask me why, we didn't want to know. We were just glad Everett wasn't around the club and Marty so much."

"Did Marty mention posing for Moony?"

"Sure. At first, he was taking portfolio shots for her music career. Later she told me she was making money posing for nude shots. I didn't think much about it one way or the other until she showed me some. Well, you saw them.

It was about that time Althea came to me, worried about her brother. He was staying out nights and he was changing, getting a big head. She feared it was drugs, and asked would we keep him out of the club. I said we would try, but she knew we were closing for the summer. When I found out he was hanging with John and Marty, doing their after-hours business, I asked Marty to try and chase Everett home. She just laughed. He was making money too, she said. Posing. Maybe more."

"What do you mean by more?"

She blew smoke toward the ceiling. "I don't know exactly. Maybe getting paid to do it. Some people will pay to watch, you know. Others, maybe to take part."

"Did you ever think of shutting Moony down?"

"And risk alienating not only Marty but Everett too? Why? Look, Jack, I'm no fan of porn. I think it's for children. But I saw no reason to interfere in something that was working fine for everyone involved. They were all adults and they had no problem with making money the way they did. Who am I to judge, much less deny them a chance to make a halfway-decent living on this pile of rocks? It wouldn't have stopped them even if I did."

"Have you heard from Everett?"

She shook her head, eyes welling up—over the loss of Everett or Marty, I couldn't tell.

I slipped behind her and held her. These were case people to me. Try as I might to know them from the papers, the photos and the corpses they left behind, in the end I never would. I could only see them objectively. For Jen, they were friends, lovers, real people with both good qualities and bad, like the rest of us. She could only see them subjectively, and for that she held the short end of the stick.

"What do I tell Abby, Jack?" Her overflowing eyes looked up at me as she pulled my hands down to hold her. "She's worried sick."

"I can't help you there."

We spent a moment that way. How can a world look so beautiful and feel so ugly? Hypothetically, that is. I haven't cared in so long I don't remember what caring feels like. It's all vanilla to me now. Hopeless vanilla.

I kissed her platinum hair and squeezed her hands.

"Gotta go," I whispered.

The girls were sitting up now, full frontal. What a world. I smiled at them as Jen walked me to the door, Lucien bouncing along behind us.

I could always find time for a kiss, especially the kind she gave, the kind that left you wanting more.

The *Jackie Oh!* was an oven and the phone was ringing as I stepped through the front door. I don't dive for it anymore.

"Dodge," I said, feeling beads of sweat form on my scalp.

"Bingo." It was Nash. "We've got to talk. You about to crash?"

"No. Name it."

"Halfway? Island Woman?"

"See you in fifteen."

I had designated the Island Woman bar as my personal line of demarcation between the contiguous United States and the Lower Keys. Dark and windowless, the place had that border feel about it. It was where farther ended and too far began.

Loo beat me there. Her Crown Vic kind of classed up the coral-rock lot. We took a deuce next to the saltwater aquarium and ordered a couple joes.

I showed her the two prints I'd lifted and briefed her on Moony's porn portfolio, as well as my morning chat with Jen. If she read any intimacy into that exchange, she kept it to herself. She did pay particular attention to Jen's responses, though, asking me to repeat her words at several points.

I watched as she unpacked dozens of manila folders onto the high-gloss nautical wooden table.

"Bank notes?"

"Trust me, Jack, you're going to like this one."

Shoving our utensils aside, Nash removed the rubber bands and started sorting the papers into piles.

My mind was still back on Jen's sundeck, wondering what on earth might have developed—and what on earth had, for that matter. Lesbians have always seemed completely logical and not particularly erotic to me. I agree with their taste in partners, after all, I just don't find two females together very arousing. Now throw a man in the mix, you've got possibilities. Lots of them. The kind that put into question great physical laws, i.e., you can't be two places at once. The Tallahassee twins and I would beg to differ. Not that such physics-defying adventures have been the norm for me. Since losing M., it's rare enough that I find one person I can halfway stand, much less two, or three.

Sarah, I can stand. As a fellow cop, as a person, maybe more, who knows? Sometimes just the uniform turns me on.

I don't know how much of that is residue of M. So far I haven't had the guts to find out.

"Stack one, the girl. Stack two, Moony. Stack three, Danswaller. You and me, we never saw Danswaller's stack, agreed?"

I nodded. He was still technically alive. Rick seemed to think so, anyway. I looked questioningly at a fourth stack.

"We'll get to that," she promised.

She unfolded the top account statement in the Marty Orleans stack and laid it out in front of me.

"Martina Orlovsky made these deposits to her bank in Kendall over the first six months of the year. Here, in March, are the first checks from PNB Newsstand Services, drawn on a Miami bank. You can follow them, every two weeks. Girl was hand-to-mouth most of that time, judging by the deposit dates anyway. The few other checks sprinkled in there are a few club dates she didn't get rich at."

She spread out a similar statement from a Key West bank, Everett Danswaller's account.

"Danswaller started at the cold storage here, in January. His deposit dates stayed pretty close to the bone too, most of this time. Same Miami bank checks."

She unfolded John Moony's financial life before my tired eyes.

"Moony opened this account in March. Not much happens until May, but here's where it starts to get interesting, Jack. Right here, in the middle of May, Moony begins regular weekly deposits of cash, three to five hundred at a pop. He's also receiving unemployment checks from Ohio, as you can see. Now look at Orlovsky and

Danswaller. Similar activity during the same period. Orlovsky's depositing three to five a week, Danswaller's more sporadic, ones and twos at a time. Again, nothing on paper, just currency."

"Fits what we know so far," I said. "Porn pays. In cash."

"Right. Now check this." She took a ledger from the fourth stack and unfolded only the bottom two-thirds of the page. "These withdrawals were made on a consistent basis the Fridays prior to the weekly deposits by our three players. In each case, if you add across, the withdrawals always exceed the combined weekly deposit by the same amount Danswaller was getting."

I nodded. "Same thing in vanilla."

"That'd be my guess, too. The other boy-toy."

"So who's big daddy?"

She turned the top of the statement over: "Account activity of: A. & J. Wilde d/b/a Puss 'n' Boots, Inc."

I brought the sheet closer. There were plenty of other entries as well, the kind that leave you recounting the zeros.

"They're pretty flush for bar owners," Loo said.

I checked the beginning and ending balances. They were making money all right. Too much of it.

"You getting that deep-down country-fresh smell, Jack?"

"Yeah, but whose laundry are they scrubbing?"

"Thought you'd never ask. Look at this."

She handed me a multi-page account summary from a New Jersey S&L. Monthly disbursements were computer-highlighted in yellow. Zeros again, lots of them. Sarah flipped the page to the checking statement. There were no corresponding drafts issued in those amounts. There also was no account name on the statement.

"I give. Who's this?"

"Our friends in Organized Crime, covering their little pinstriped butts. That's just one small report on PNB Newsstand Services. OC is building a case around cartel money and they don't exactly want it shared with country bumpkins like us. My contact tells me there are a couple dozen scrub houses operating up and down the coast, Puss 'n' Boots being one of the most recent. PNB Newsstand is a legitimate enterprise. It only serves as a conduit for the other stuff. Oh, and did I mention it's my ass if OC hears we've so much as split an empanada on Calle Ocho?"

"But if they're involved…"

Nash shook her head.

"You remember Ray Cruz, back in the game? He's working as missing-persons liaison with OC on the racketeering case. OC told me to call him. Ray swears the PNB operation is legit. Mob, but legit. He says whatever happened came out of our end, that PNB wouldn't know or care whether Martina Orlovsky lived or died, much less risk doing anything about it. Says it would be like blowing a fly off your head with a shotgun."

"Apt analogy this week. Tell me I'm blind, but we've got zip on paper tying the Wilde sisters to PNB Newsstand?"

"You got it, Jack. We can make a pretty good circumstantial case, based on the dates of the cash deposits and withdrawals, linking them financially to Moony's porn operation. Which brings up the question of why they're trying to hide that, and what more they may be keeping from us. We can even speculate that the money out of Jersey was being washed, rinsed and line-dried in the process. But like you said, porn pays cash, and cash doesn't leave much of a trail."

I thought about Jen from every angle as my Jeep rambled back to the rock. I just couldn't put her, or us, in a spot. She was several bubbles to the wild side, sure. She never would have bothered with me otherwise. She had allowed me glimpses of her that might only be seen in certain lights, under certain conditions, like iridescent orchids. I found some warmth in there where I was least expecting it, a scared little girl wearing a grown-up's remarkably smooth skin.

But was there a liar in there? Or worse?

I couldn't be sure.

And I was a little worried at what it might cost to find out.

Chapter 16
The Boneyard

Each summer, Jonah becomes a permanent fixture at Blue Heaven, blissfully enjoying its outdoor dining and relaxed rhythms without the running commentary of Bob and Shirley Slaphappy from Bucktooth Falls, Ohio. I like the joint, too. A little upscale for my tastes maybe, but very Conch nonetheless, from the free-roaming cats and chickens underfoot to the wild green parrots in the overhanging banyans.

Heaven has a delightfully goofy past. It was once a boxing ring where Papa actually threw a few lefts. It was a brothel. It even played host to island cockfights at one time. A little rooster graveyard with tough little tombstones pays homage to the scrappy birds that managed to fight their way out of the broiler.

The lackadaisical waitstaff always seated us at the same distant garden table and left us alone to awaken at a civilized pace, Jonah with his beloved *New York Times* crossword puzzle, I with bits and pieces of my previous evening, which I would attempt to fit together like Lego blocks to make something of myself.

A half-dozen Hemingway clones were already seated nearby. You couldn't get away from them this week. They were everywhere: bars, restaurants, mopeds, bikes, charter boats. Making their pilgrimages to anyplace the old man might have pissed or passed out, and he most certainly did both at Blue Heaven. This pack of Papas was relatively well behaved. Still, I found their presence a constant reminder of the case I wasn't solving. I smoked more and ate less.

Calls to Jen that afternoon had proven futile. Likewise to her sister, Abby, and the club itself. I held on to a thread of hope that it could all be explained, the cash coming and going, all those zeros, apparently taking in laundry and paying for porn. Sure, Jen was no angel. Angels don't come to Key Weird. But there was a big difference between making a living and making a killing and the Conch in me has a permanent bad attitude when it comes to big money. Chalk that up to generations of just scraping by on a rock where even the coral has given up. Live and let live is the island way, but die and let die…well, it's not quite that simple. Not for me.

Briefing Michaels had been like talking to the Wailing Wall. In Rick World, his case was already made six ways from Sunday and he was treating himself to a night off as a reward. Never avoid the obvious, he kept parroting into the phone. That's what they teach you in academy and he was a textbook guy if there ever was one. You want to close a case, build on the evidence you have, son, not on the evidence you don't. Hit a sixteen, hold a seventeen, regardless. Don't take chances. Don't play hunches.

Only experience can undo that kind of training—if you're lucky, before it kills you.

Me, I had enough loose ends to hang myself. All I was really sure of was that I had to get to Everett Danswaller before Swingin' Dick did, and I had to get Jen to level with me. Little did I know both my wishes were about to come true, after a fashion. Memo to myself: Be careful what you wish for.

I could tell by the way Jonah refolded the *Citizen* that the puzzle had gotten the best of him. John Moony's mug shot stared up at me from page one. On this rock, he was now officially burnt toast. Dead men don't hire lawyers to beat a murder rap. The accompanying story featured more of the same hardboiled manhunt lingo Rick loved to spout. Catch the Bahamian, day two. But like Jonah's crossword, there were still a few blank squares. I might not have the answers yet, but I was beginning to see where they crossed.

"Your twins stopped by, after the two of you left," Jonah mentioned casually.

"Is that your way of saying I told you so?" He'd already heard about my night and day.

"She really is so lovely."

"Mmm."

"So where does it go from here, star-crossed lovers? It's all very Dashiell Hammett, you know."

"Don't remind me."

"I found them quite charming in a my-sister-was-really-my-mother, Southern gothic sort of way."

"They can tie two cherry stems together with their tongues," I said.

"Fascinating."

"I think I should have stayed in Tallahassee."

"What, and miss the sweet torment of unrequited lesbian love?"

"You get bitter when that puzzle beats you, you know that?"

"There is always tomorrow, my dear. Like today, only better."

"Just get the check, Scarlet."

Jonah set off on his short evening constitutional to the Chameleon. He liked to sashay by Kelly's and flirt with the bartender there. He was shameless in his own refined sort of way.

I returned to the Jeep just as the street lamps came on to find a note waiting under the wiper. I unfolded it. The hand-scrawl read: "Remember the Maine. Midnight. E.D."

My first thought was, now we're getting somewhere. My second was, what is it about cemeteries and midnight?

Some of my happiest adolescent memories were born at the city boneyard. When my folks finally gave it up and I was stationed permanently aboard the *Jackie Oh!* with Max, my grandfather kept strict shrimper's hours, which left me no home options in the seduction department. My choices were a car I didn't have or the rickety un-godly-comfortable skiff. The girl's place was no good, either. Conch-house walls are so thin, they barely keep the wind out.

Then a wonderfully earthy Cuban girl introduced me to the romantic possibilities of the cemetery. It was great: the stars, the quiet, the warm cement beneath us, all fenced in and private. I soon became something of a connoisseur of crypts. Some were tall with a view, some were low and intimate, some were even covered in case of rain.

Depending on your partner, the right crypt could make all the difference.

Some of my friends thought it was perverse and ghoulish, but then they had cars. You want perverse, try getting anything but a good groin pull for your trouble in a leaky wooden skiff.

I hadn't been back to the cemetery since Max passed, but I remembered his simple grass plot and tombstone. Not a place I would have chosen to do it, in any case.

I parked the Jeep on Angela and walked along the cemetery side, looking for breaches in the cyclone fence. I knew as well as Everett Danswaller there were any number of ways in. The place was almost as well visited after-hours as it was in daylight. Teenage lovers, stoners, and various voodoo and Santeria characters working their mojos and practicing their gris-gris made for a lively blend of altered realities on any given night. Add the intoxicating smell of the night-blooming cereus cactus and the overripe tropical moon, and it was quite easy to imagine all sorts of apparitions, spooks, ghosts and zombies wandering the place, too. Spend a little time there and believe me, dead is not a word you would use to describe the Key Weird cemetery.

I stooped through a sizable opening in the fence. The summer grass was dry and crackled as I stepped over it and onto one of the avenues that crisscross the fifteen-acre worm farm. The place was ancient by American standards, a hundred-fifty years old at least. Nobody knows how many bodies reside here, many of them in aboveground mausoleums made popular before there were tools to dig through the solid coral rock two feet down. Afterlife census estimates range into six figures, four times the breathing population and a lot more polite.

I stopped in the shadows between two shrines and lit up, catching a glance at my watch in the match light. Nearly midnight.

Some years had passed, and some people too, since I knew this place well. Walking farther, I finally got my bearings and set course in the general direction of Popeye the drunken sailor. Well, that's what we called him. The statue of a seaman, his left hand shielding his eyes, was meant to be peering out to sea in search of his departed shipmates, lost when the battleship Maine went down in Havana Harbor. In our young and skewed experience, sailors were always looking for the same thing in Key Weird, and it wasn't their fallen comrades. Hence the nickname.

I saw the white military markers and the silhouette of old Popeye toward the end of the lane. I crushed my smoke and slipped the safety off my .45. Reflexes bent my knees and slowed my pace. I moved cautiously off to the side of the path, out of potential sightlines. My topsiders crunched coral-rock. Adrenaline began to fill my gut like a firehose. My heartbeat was pounding in my ears.

Thirty feet from the Maine memorial, I sensed movement and froze, listening hard. A hand appeared from behind the monument, palm toward me. I crouched and held aim.

"Mr. Dodge?" came the whisper from behind the granite.

I didn't reply.

Part of a head peered out in silhouette.

"Don't shoot."

"Give me a reason not to."

"I'm unarmed, you know. I've got information. I'm not the one they lookin' for." He had the shakes. Bad.

I held on him and moved right, off onto the brittle summer grass.

"Then why'd you run?" I still couldn't see him.

"Who you think they believe?"

"Why should I believe you?"

"'Cos you know I didn't do it already. You know that much."

"What's the plan here, Everett? How you going to play this?"

"I got two things to tell you. Do what you can before they catch me, maybe everything be cool."

"I'm all ears."

I could hear him breathing.

"You know John Moony, yes? John didn't kill Marty."

"How do you know she's dead?"

"Little bird told me."

"How do you know Moony wasn't involved?"

"She was making him rich, you know. Why would he kill her?"

"Some think you put him up to it."

"That bullshit. Marty and me were tight."

"But not tight enough? You wanted more, right?"

"At first, sure. Before John. After, I didn't want no more. Wasn't no more to want, you know?"

"If you're dealing straight with me, then who killed Marty?"

"Man, you think I wouldn't tell you, I knew that?"

"What about Moony?"

"Same thing."

"Why'd you skip work yesterday?"

There was a pause. I could hear the fear as he struggled to breathe.

"I knew something bad going down. That's all I can say now."

"Who's the other boy-toy in the pictures?"

"That's the other thing. I'm afraid of him. He moves with the Hemingways. That's how John got into that. But him a wolf in sheep's clothing. If he killed them, he looking to kill me, too."

"A name, Everett. Give me a name."

"You know him…"

I saw two explosions, like tiny meteors, burst from the granite side of the Maine memorial before I heard the muffled shots. Out of my left peripheral vision, I saw the dark figure of Everett Danswaller moving fast and low through the obstacle course of mausoleums and tombstones, running for his life.

I spun right. For a split second, I saw the ghost of Ernest Hemingway frozen in the moonlight, his distinctive beard a brilliant white against facial features darkened by the brim of a billed fishing cap. He did not hesitate to spit a muffled shot at my head. Instinct sent me diving away from my eternal rest behind a marble gravestone.

I scrambled to my knees and cautiously peeked to the side of my headstone to see the gunman sprinting after Danswaller. I hurried my pace in pursuit, but by the time I reached the closest hole in the fence they were gone.

Back at the Jeep, blood had saturated the left shoulder of my shirt and I knew Papa hadn't entirely missed his mark. In the rearview, I could see a small flap of skin where my earlobe and jaw would normally meet.

The ER crew took one look at me, assumed the usual and stitched me up without even breaking their conversation.

A party was in full swing aboard the *Popinjay* as I pulled alongside Houseboat Row. I'd been to a couple, just to be neighborly. I preferred my drinks straight up, without the chatter. I would be preferring one directly, with codeine.

I'd just slipped the key in the lock when I smelled her French cut.

"In early," she said.

I could see her silhouette now, in the hammock, as I turned the key.

"Drink?"

"Whatever you're having."

I stripped off my bloody shirt and built us Manhattans. Fresh cigarette between my lips, I carried the drinks onto the deck and handed her one.

"Lost souls," I said.

We touched rims.

"What happened?" She rubbed her earlobe.

"Oh. Too close a shave."

"Everett called me today."

"Mmm. How is he?"

"Fairly scared, I'd say. He knew about John. I told him about Marty."

The nectar of the gods was unlocking my codeine threes. I just waited, waited and enjoyed.

"Jack, I'm…I haven't been trying to deceive you, but I haven't…"

"You're working." My best impression.

She grinned. "I deserved that."

"Shall we try that Moony thing again?"

She sighed, fidgeting in the hammock, forced to recite.

"Abby and I, we sort of divide the business, you know. Abby does the books, I meet and greet. The last couple seasons, I've wanted to close down in the summer and travel, but Abby wouldn't go for it. With our overhead, even doing half-business in the summer helps financially. And she's right, we have some money in trusts, but we're not swimming in it. It was Marty who came to us with the solution. She and John cooked it up. Marty was driving for that company. Along with *Time* and *Newsweek*, she was also delivering porn magazines, the really crude newspaper type. You probably know all that. Anyway, she met the guys behind the porn papers. Marty, she'd try anything twice, three times if it paid."

"She hadn't met Moony at that point?"

Jen shook her head.

"Not until she discovered the Point. Marty sat-in there a couple times and Moony was in the audience shooting pictures. Pretty soon, she brought him around. She knew Abby and I couldn't agree on closing the place, so she worked the angles."

"With her as the go-between."

"Yes. The porn guys had her put Moony's film in a locked mail pouch each week and she'd drive it back to Miami on her run. The next week, she would return with the mail sack filled with cash for the photos. Abby would count the money, subtract our share, then pay them all in cash from our business account. The business withdrawals we planned to write off as promoting Marty's career."

"Turning a tidy little summer profit from a closed club," I said.

"Don't be judgmental." She turned sullen, commiserating with her drink.

"It must have seemed like a winner all around."

She shrugged, the frightened little girl again. If she knew I wasn't buying, she didn't let on.

"What can you do for Everett? I can't believe he's mixed up in any of this." Her eyes watched me from the rim of her glass.

"He seems to be doing fairly well on his own, so far. What did he tell you?"

"He asked me to look in on Althea and the kids."

"Didn't mention any travel plans?"

"He didn't say. Where's he going to go from here, huh?"

"Pretty much," I agreed.

We finished our drinks. She was an easy carry to the master cabin.

Chapter 17
Pete's Warning

"Now you're it."

Pete had a point, even if I didn't want to admit it.

Nash was sitting in the armchair with a case file this thick on her lap, dress uniform, her wild hair now pulled neatly back and pinned. I was leaning, one leg up on the worktable, downing lousy squad room joe like it was Dom.

We'd been over the evening's developments a couple times already, except for the part about a certain platinum blond Goldilocks sleeping in my bed. I guess I didn't want Nash to get all goosey about it and I didn't want the chief to think I was that stupid.

Pete was hounding his way through the finer points of what the lab rats and I had retrieved from the boneyard on first light. In less than an hour, we'd managed to match the construction shoe prints from the truck, dig the bullet that grazed me out of a tree and bag a few synthetic white fibers from the hole in the fence that seemed to indicate the gunman may not be all that attached to his beard.

Pete didn't like it. Not one bit.

"You talk to the kid yet?" Meaning Rick.

"Not since all this. There was no getting through to him yesterday."

"Puts me in a hell of a bind, Jack, after going their way on this."

What could I say?

Pete pushed up from his chair with a grunt and refilled his joe. Nash set her paper doorstop aside and went to the dry board to sketch out our dismal situation in happy primary colors.

"OK. The killer is after Danswaller, to tie up loose ends somehow. So far as we know, he hasn't gotten him. Danswaller is after you, Jack. You're his only hope. The killer also somehow knows this and follows you, figuring you'll lead him to Danswaller. And you do, but Danswaller escapes. Now the killer has two problems: he doesn't know how much Danswaller told you and he doesn't know how good a look you got at him. Which means the killer still needs you alive, since you're his best hope of finding Danswaller. Once he does the Bahamian, you would be next."

"Which brings us to the festival, Jack," Pete took the lead. "I know your Hemingways judging starts tonight, but much as I endorse our little summer celebration, I have no intention of placing an officer in jeopardy because of it. You know the choices here as well as I do, Jack. And you probably know I don't like any of them."

I lit a smoke. Pete knew when I was just watching his lips move and it made him all colicky.

"Jack, I want you to step down as a judge," he said, all calm and businesslike.

I just smoked and looked at him. Nash shifted uneasily in her chair.

"You're just too visible a target, Jack. Wouldn't be any point trying to back you up. It'd be worthless."

He took my silence for noncompliance and simmered a moment before pressing on.

"You think I like this? I want this guy as bad as you do. But he's in control here and he has every reason to see your ass dead."

I killed my coffee.

He leaned forward and gave me his hardest hard look. I wouldn't want to be one of his boys in these father-son situations.

"And I did not pull your sorry ass out of the fire just so you could cowboy yourself into a grave over some dirty pictures! How am I going to live with that?"

We both knew what came next. Getting dangerously close to M. territory. Not a place either of us went if there were any other destinations left to choose.

"Look, Pete, I appreciate the concern. Honestly. But Loo forgot one thing up there. She forgot to list what Jack wants. And along with peace on earth and a chilled Manhattan, I want to see this twist-o on the far end of a cellblock. Now the way I see it, if things go right, the festival could end up bringing Papa to me. The look-alike contest is exactly where he's going to be hiding, watching and waiting. That getup is probably how he managed to trail me so far in the first place. Like Loo says, he's not going to try anything, especially in a crowd, until Danswaller contacts me again."

"If he's still alive," Loo reminded me.

Pete glanced her way, took off his Buddy Hollys and rubbed his eyes. He looked older than when we started all this.

"You two work things out with the kid first," he mumbled, as if to no one.

Too bad. I was listening now.

Loo lugged her paper case. I caught the office door for her.

"And Jack?"

I turned, not quite removing the half-grin from my face in time.

"Don't become that great guy who used to work here."

Nash let her hair go over Seven Mile Bridge as we flew toward the storm that awaited us on the rock.

"How does this judging work, Jack?"

It was her first Hemingway Days.

"Well, they call it a look-alike contest, but there's actually more to it than that. These guys recite bits of Hemingway's writing sometimes, tell stories, sing songs, you name it, all over a lot of beer at Sloppy's. Which is why the judging is spread over two nights. Lorian tells me we've got eighty-three Papas entered this year. We'll pare it down to a dozen or so tonight, then the final round determines the winner tomorrow night, after the parade."

"How'd you draw the duty?"

"It's a long story."

I enjoyed her hair blowing everywhere. It felt a little like it used to with M. sitting beside me, bare feet wiggling against the dash, keeping time with the salsa station as we drove, laughing and baking in the hot Florida sun. None of that with Loo, of course. Uniformed, buttoned-down Loo. Just the hair. The hair was the same.

I dropped her by the *Jackie Oh!* On my way into town. She had her change of clothes with her and the use of my Cuban special two-wheeler for the day. No need to lock a pieced-together heap like that. Guess that's why we call them specials.

Michaels was unusually dapper in gray trops, maroon pinstripe button-down, four-in-hand rep tie and coordinated suspenders over his shoulder holster. He waved me back to his corner sanctum.

"County Jack."

"Swingin'."

I helped myself to his pot of joe.

Bottom line, Rick wouldn't budge on his airtight case against Danswaller, despite my aching ear and the story that came with it. Of course Danswaller is going to say Moony is innocent now that he's dead, Rick figured, the better to save his own ass. And any number of people could be after Danswaller now, for any number of reasons. There was no hard evidence to tie the shooter to the other crimes, only that same handful of loose ends I kept mentioning. Besides, if the girl's killer had a soft gun, why'd he go to the trouble of removing her head? Or frying Moony? Why not just cap them? Unfortunately, I didn't have my answer book handy.

"What else did Danswaller tell you, anyway?" Rick asked, scratching notes on a yellow legal pad.

I thought that one over and responded carefully.

"He said he was scared of the other boy-toy. From the photos."

"Did you get a name?" he asked without looking up.

"I know him."

That wrapped up his note-taking abruptly.

If I held out any hopes that Rick might volunteer to join us at Sloppy's, they were quickly dashed. I might as well have been speaking Esperanto for all the response it brought from Swingin' Dick.

Our curious exchange played on my mind as I drove home along Smathers Beach. I could never be certain of my true motivation when I went with a hunch like that. I didn't want to share information about Danswaller with Rick for obvious reasons: I thought the man was innocent, while Rick was intent on reserving him a ride on Old Sparky up in Starketown. Clearly, the unknown boy-toy was one of the ragged loose ends he would rather not deal with. He could only mess up Rick's case, so why pursue it?

Still, something in my gut, some private gris-gris, told me to hold back. I didn't understand why at first. Perhaps it might prove useful in some unforeseen circumstances to appear to have an edge on Rick, even if neither of us knew for certain who the fourth for Strip Poker had been.

Nash was gone with my bike when I pulled up to the *Jackie Oh!* Horst, the bald one, was busy making repairs to one of the *Popinjay's* shore lines.

"Hello, Jack. Your friend just left."

"I know. Thanks. Listen, I was talking to Jurgen the other day about Puss 'n' Boots."

"Yes. He is still upset they are closed."

"I know. He said you had seen Jen and Marty around, clubbing."

"Sometimes, yes."

"Have you ever seen them with another man? Maybe a friend?"

"You mean besides the schwartzer?"

"Besides him."

"I've seen them with Ricky a couple times, yes. You know Ricky?"

I had him describe Swingin' Dick to me.

"And there was the photographer. Do you know him? From the Point?"

"I didn't know him."

"Yes. I heard. Terrible."

"When you saw them with Ricky, did they dance together, the three of them, or did they pair off?"

Horst thought a moment.

"I think they danced one to one, not all together. Ricky is more like the middle brother to them, I think. In-between Jen and Marty."

I thanked him and filed the information under Loose Ends. Swingin' Dick never mentioned he knew Marty or the Wilde sisters socially. Then again, I guess I never asked. It's a small island. On any given case, Rick is probably no more than two phone calls away from the killer. The trick is knowing which two.

Inside, I washed down two more C3s with a hastily concocted Manhattan. I needed to think and sleep, in no particular order.

Chapter 18
Ricky

I had M. back in my arms again, right here in Key Weird aboard the *Jackie Oh!* It was a dream of course and I was aware of that and clung to it, even as the sensations we choose to call real finally penetrated and destroyed the far better universe of my own imagining.

M. was the consummate professional, both on and off the job. She carried herself at a certain angle toward life the way a tree will grow toward the sunlight and away from the shade. Which is not to say she lacked for personality. Quite the contrary, she had a natural charm and a quick wit, and could kick both up to actual effervescence when circumstances called for it. She was funny, she was caring, she was sensual, she was relaxed and engaging, and somehow she brought those same qualities out in others. Which is the long way of saying she was many things I am not.

As I got to know her better, I discovered another fascinating side to her that she kept hidden, certainly from her employers, but also from friends and even family who thought they knew her well. It had to do with the way she approached her job, or rather how we approached the job, for it would become our secret sharing. Somehow, things always had a way of circling back to the job.

At a certain level in law enforcement, you go from chasing the sociopaths to working alongside them. I'm not saying all Homicide dicks are potential killers, any more than I'd say all federal agents have what it takes to run flake. But there reaches a point in studying the criminal mind where any intelligent cop begins to appreciate the aesthetics of the well-crafted heist, the near-perfect murder, the ingenious drug scam. That's where you cross the line from law enforcement into what M. and I shared, out on some terra nova beyond the limited concepts of good and evil or right and wrong. It was a way of coping with the madness by studying the aesthetics of it rather than labeling and dismissing it out of hand. Crime criticism is what it was.

In the squad room, at the shop, you could be as cynical as you pleased in the day to day, no one would bat an eye or think less of you so long as you never questioned who the good guys were. Back home in the Grove, however, or jogging along Biscayne, or flying up ninety-five on weekends, we committed that cardinal sin, our little indulgence, the better to view our cases from all sides. Crime is far richer and more satisfying if you aren't rooting for a home team. M. taught me that.

Nights and weekends, we found ourselves actually reviewing our cases the same way a critic might review a movie. How was the acting? The directing? The screenplay? Did the costumes work? Were the extras believable? For every crime worthy of real detective work, there were a hundred that you could only rank as B-movies: shaky plots, misdirected, poorly cast, badly lit, with endings you could see for miles. Any good crime critic would have walked out on them. The ones we loved were the ones our superiors loathed, the Oscar contenders, cases masterfully constructed to stand up to the most intense police scrutiny. Two thumbs up, way up, on those.

And like all critics, I guess we longed to direct, sure. It may seem farfetched, a Homicide detective and a federal agent holding hands, walking along the beach, plotting to, say, kill a visiting foreign dignitary. But it was a rich and real part of our life together, sometimes more real than the job. I would say something like, "How do you think it could have been pulled off?" and away we'd go.

Sure, we got paid to solve crimes, not commit them, but the exercise helped us stay connected intellectually, gave us distance from the minutiae of our work and kept our cynicism in check. Good and bad are just two shades, after all. We wanted to view this life in Technicolor, M. and me.

We loved and respected each other so completely, as cops and human beings, I guess deep inside we both knew we would somehow find a way to work a case together.

Sadly, very sadly, we did.

I rose, lost and alone and badly out of shape for all this. M. should be here, I told myself, running this killer to ground, not me. She had the sharper mind. She was always one step ahead of me.

The twins had called while I was on the nod. So had Lorian, checking in to apologize for her flamer. And Jonah, summoning me to a Cuban breakfast.

I shaved carefully and applied a less conspicuous flesh-colored bandage to my do-it-yourself face-lift. Black and blue was settling in. Then I threw on my outriggers, topsiders and Papa tee shirt, gunned a C3 for the road and coasted down Flagler to El Siboney.

The closest thing to Havana this side of the Straits of Florida, El Siboney is the real deal, a family-run Cuban diner that sends as much food out the door takeout as to the tables. The waitresses in their red shirts and black slacks chew gum and call you Honey. They all look like they have a half-dozen screaming mouths at home and haven't slept since the Bay of Pigs.

Jonah was wedged into a corner deuce, working his daily amid the clamor.

"Lead with your head again?" he greeted me, barely glancing up.

I gave him the top of the news over a café Cubano.

"So our Mr. Danswaller lives."

"Last time I saw him."

"And one very bad Papa remains at large, apparently."

"Jonah, can I ask you about Swingin' Dick."

He put the *Citizen* down and gave me a look.

"What about him?"

"That's just it, I'm not sure. What do you know about him, OTR."

"Off the record? Oh, dear me, you work with him, Jack."

"He's acting a little strange on this one. I just want your take."

"I see him around. He's a big fan, as you know. Aren't they all, kiss kiss?"

"Where do you see him most?"

"Shores. Epoch. Sometimes he comes in to see the show."

"Who does he club with?"

He gave me his best patronizing-bitch look.

"Oh, I see. This is a little lover's tiff, is it?"

"Spare me."

"Well, yes, now that you mention it, I have seen him with your fair lady lesbian friend on occasion. I don't think there is much to worry about there, do you?"

"What about with a tall black man?"

"Meaning your missing Bahamian, I suppose?"

"OK."

"I have seen him with a number of men, black and white," he said. "Including you, I might add."

"Let's try this another way."

"What are you really looking for, Jack?"

"Gossip. Rumors. Innuendo."

"Well, you do know Ricky, don't you? Party boy. Good dancer. I hear he likes a little rough trade on occasion. Just hearsay, mind you. He's not too out-there publicly, I imagine because of his boss. And he always dresses well, doesn't he?"

"He does. Is he men-only? Men and women?"

"I have no idea and I don't plan to find out, thank you."

"But you see him with both."

"I see you with twins."

"It's not a judgment thing, I'm just trying…"

"Our Ricky has the worst disease there is, Jack. He's young. Maybe he's running away from something, maybe he's running from himself. They're a dime a dozen in this town and they're all just like us. They don't party this hard because they're well-adjusted and happy, you know."

Agreed. But it didn't explain what was eating Rick.

I gave Jen a call. No luck.

I decided to try Swingin' on his cell phone.

"Richard Michaels." And a lot of party-noise static.

"Let's talk about the Wilde sisters. Where are you."

"No can do, bud. I'm sucking down Mai Tais on the sunset cruise, Big Johnny's treatski. Can't it wait?"

"When you back?"

"I don't know. Late, probably. Listen, if it's urgent…"

"Nothing that can't wait. Leave a message on my machine later if you land somewhere, OK?"

"You got it, bud."

Jonah was polishing off the last of his flan when I returned.

"I see where you're headed with this," he said. "The mystery boy-toy."

"Rick thinks he's got a case against Danswaller and won't see anything else. I've got plenty of things that don't fit right, and one of them is, I'm beginning to think Rick's not telling me everything he knows."

"Tricky situation," he agreed. "Him having it all solved and all."

Sloppy Joe's was already a madhouse when I arrived, partiers and Papas spilling out onto Duval and Greene from the old weathered archways. A trio was gamely playing, but the general racket reduced their efforts to more of an annoying electric scratching than actual music. The sunbaked concrete and brick of Old Town was holding onto the summer heat. Beer was sloshing everywhere. The college coed behind the tee shirt concession looked like a frightened caged animal.

Lorian, standing on a chair, spotted me and flagged me in like a runway jockey. The judge's stand was front and center. She ran introductions to my fellow judges, two of whom I recognized from last year and two new ones. I didn't catch any of their names for the clamor.

Once the formalities were concluded, the contest began in earnest, or more precisely, Ernest. The judging would take about two hours, if I remembered last year with anything approaching accuracy, after which I would likely stagger off into the night with a ringing in my ears and a slight manic buzz from the bottomless beer.

I never cease to be bewildered by the sincerity of the look-alike contestants, many of whom return year after year, cheering section in tow, hoping to carry away the winner's trophy. They try every technique, from bleaching their facial hair, arm hair, even their chest hair, to filling their cheeks with tissues, to minor plastic surgery, all in a cockamamie attempt to resemble some long-dead literary lion. There are safari Papas and sea captain Papas and Sun Valley plaid Papas and lots of in-between Papas whose reference points are way over my head. I don't know what he talked like, I don't know what he sang like, I don't know what kind of aftershave the guy wore, but they seem to.

I have one very simple criterion by which I judge each and every entrant: does he make me want to throw a punch at him? I know as much about Hemingway as you can learn from the Cliff Notes version of *The Sun Also Rises,* but I gather he could be a cantankerous cuss and was not one to let well enough alone when in the company of drinking men. Max, who did his share of rum running during Prohibition, once told me Papa was a mean drunk who fought like a girl. So it seemed logical to me that I might well have ended up coming to blows with the big windbag myself, had our drunken paths ever chanced to cross, though he was long gone by the time I was born. If you wanted my vote, you had to make my fists clench just a little and my front teeth grate back and forth like they were getting ready to spit in your eye.

I spotted Nash a half-hour into the contest. She had a Hemingway Days baseball cap pulled down on her wild curls, making it look like one of those souvenir-shop novelty numbers that come with the big rock-star hair tacked under the brim. She was cool and observant, the way I knew she would be, and her presence made me feel a little better about breaking for a nature call.

The men's was a disaster, even by Sloppy's standards, proving once again what poor carryout containers humans make. I kept a close eye on the few Papa wannabes who were jockeying for relief alongside me. I would have happily decked several of them, that's how good the field was this year.

I wedged, shoved and jostled my way back through the human bug swarm, trying to catch some of the safari Papa on stage. He was good, but he didn't make me want to smack him, and I cast a hasty no vote when I managed to reach the judge's table. As I prepared to take my seat, I found a folded note on my chair.

"Conch Train yard. Midnight. E.D."

Chapter 19
Conch Train

Mean low tide had drawn a fetid haze over the rock. Nash drove the Jeep sober and fast, twisting and turning through the drunken narrow streets of Old Town. The moon looked like a flashlight beneath a bed sheet.

I borrowed her flip phone and dialed my number. No messages. Then I lit the smoke I figured she wanted and one for myself.

"What'd you think?" I asked, handing it to her.

"Crazy white folks."

I chuckled in agreement.

"You got a nice laugh, Jack, you know that?"

"Mmm."

"You should use that more often."

I directed her down Caroline where it feeds into Eaton, then left and out Palm. From there, it would be a straight shot to Roosevelt, where they circle the Conch Tour Trains at night.

"You didn't see anyone drop the note?"

"I was watching after you, remember?"

The judges hadn't witnessed the delivery either, intent as they were on the contestants.

"Jack, we're not going to cowboy this thing, right?"

I smoked, thinking.

"Because I'm more than happy to save your ass, you know that, so long as you're not planning on sticking it way high up in the wind. You hear me?"

"What are you carrying?"

She glared at me. "My nine."

"That's it?"

"Did you just hear me talking to you?"

I reached behind and under her seat, pulled the Velcro strap, freed my JIC and stuck it in her waistband.

"It's a Walther PPK. When you use it, think Bond, James Bond. And aim a little to the left."

The Friday night traffic noise from Roosevelt made me edgy. So did the dull ache in my jaw.

We passed by the Conch Train depot. All quiet.

Nash pulled in at a convenience store and parked off to the blind side. She wound her hair up in a spiral, tucked it under her cap and got out. With her high cheekbones and lanky model's build, she could have passed for a teenager, some kid just out hanging, looking for it. In the cover of the Jeep, she pulled the nine from her shoulder bag, double-checked the clip and released the safety. Then she gave me a look as she performed the same check on the PPK by rote, replaced it with her nine, and tucked my spare gun into the back of her shorts, cold metal against auburn brown skin. I liked the way she pointed the grip left, a two-fisted girl.

I hopped over to the driver's side and started the Jeep.

"Mind yourself now, you hearin' me? I am in no mood to give blood tonight."

I grinned and rubbed my bandaged ear.

"Don't worry, Loo. He's a terrible shot."

I pulled onto Roosevelt and drove as far as Sears Town to give her some walking time, then circled back and parked in front of the Conch Train depot, feeling my valves tighten down fast. A quick check of my own weapon helped calm me. So did seeing Nash moseying along, a bagged bottle swinging freely in her left hand. She'd worked Vice at Metro. Must be like riding a bike, that walk.

She wandered past me with the look and sang out an incoherent street greeting that quickly turned sour and obscene. I ignored her. She moved far away from the traffic lights, finally seating herself for a party of one in the caboose car of a deserted tourist train.

I scanned the Conch Train yard for signs of movement. There was no way of knowing whether Nash had been noticed and overlooked as the random Key Weird passerby or had scotched the meet by her presence. Walking on was the only way to find out.

I held my .45 at my side and stepped over the chain and into the yard. There must have been a dozen of the street trains, happy yellow mock engines with two, three, four awning-covered passenger cars in tow. You saw them around town so often that you ceased to see them at all, like the cats and New Jersey plates.

I glanced in Loo's direction. She was slouched down low in her cartoon train car. I knew the top would still be on that bottle when this was all over.

The sides of the passenger cars were open and offered minimum cover, but the engines were broad and bulky and another story. I moved slowly and carefully beside the engines and quickly between the cars, feeling the oily asphalt squish beneath my topsiders with every step.

I was midway into the circled wagons when a single bright flash dead ahead blinded me. I moved low and left behind a train car, trying to get a bearing on the nearest engine. I had only peripheral vision, and barely that.

I could hear the whirring sound of a flash recharging. There was motion off to my right, maybe Nash, maybe not.

I made for the nearest engine and dove behind it as the light flashed again and just as quickly faded, leaving only blackness and my partial blindness.

I was pinned. I couldn't risk a look even if I could see and I couldn't risk another move, not until my vision cleared. Just one problem: I didn't dare stay put, either.

I was beginning to make out silhouettes in my field of vision, but hearing was still my better ally. I could track my pursuer by the high-pitched whir of the flash pack—until it was recharged, that is.

He seemed to be circling to my left, away from the motion I hoped was my backup. From where I crouched now, I might make him out with the aid of the streetlights off Roosevelt, if I could manage a peek without frying my retinas.

The flash burned the night again, this time directed slightly away from me.

Nash.

The whirring again, moving right now. I scrambled to the rear of the engine, keeping it between the battery sound and my recovering vision.

Then I had a grim thought: If my backup is blind, I would have to be her backup now. And I didn't like hearing the hurried movements of the whirring man, like he was onto the kill.

My vision was coming, but I didn't dare wait for it to clear any further. I drew a bead on the next engine ahead and scrambled toward it.

Off to the left, I saw enough of a silhouette to recognize the old fisherman's cap and beard. Then the flash turned my path to daylight and I heard the first muffled report from the silencer digging holes in the air around me.

I skidded to a stop behind the engine and checked myself for leaks.

Papa knew exactly where I was now. From his angle, I might as well be in Fastbuck Freddy's window with a neon arrow pointing this way. I could not pin him down as precisely, nor did I know whether Nash was blinded or merely being patient, waiting for my play. But I didn't like the flash-and-fire combination, not one bit.

I could have used a good icebreaker from M. She had a real knack for them in situations like this. Me, I usually went with the moment.

"I'm hit, I'm hit!" I yelled, followed by a good loud laugh, the kind Nash likes. "Seriously, my friend, you are going to injure someone with that thing one day, mark my words."

Several spits perforated the smokestack and engine house behind which I hid.

I laughed again, louder. "Listen, listen, I'll bring the cans, you bring the beer, we'll practice, practice, practice. Deal?"

More silenced rounds fell on the machinery around me.

"My friend Loo's a great shot. We'll bring her along. Right, Loo?"

There was a short pause, then I heard Sarah's voice.

"Yeah, I'll teach this motherfucker how it works."

A few rounds in Loo's direction followed.

"So listen, Papa. May I call you Papa? Or Ern? I do like Ern a little better. So listen, Ern, what'll it be? Because as you can see, Loo and me somehow seem to have ended up on either side of you, and you know how hard it is to take a good class picture that way. So I'm thinking we should just put the hardware away for now until we can get you checked out proper on all this stuff. What do you think?"

A flash suddenly bleached the haze white. I wheeled around the engine in time to catch Nash advancing in a crouched sprint toward the light source. We met at the flash unit, whirring unattended beside its recharging power pack. Nash pointed off in the distance, away from the highway, at a shadow in fast retreat.

I just shook my head.

Nash nursed a decaf nudge while I plowed the same old ground, hoping to turn up a new crop of leads. The *Jackie Oh!* Was good for rocking the adrenaline out of your system. Well after midnight, the island had finally ceased its usual roar.

There had been messages from Jen and the Tallahassee twins on my machine, but no word from Michaels. I wasn't liking what I was feeling.

"It's the phantom planet thing," I explained. "When things don't move in the proper orbit, there's usually a phantom planet you haven't seen, exerting a gravitational pull on them."

"And you think Rick's the phantom planet here?"

I knew it sounded farfetched. After all, he was a Homicide detective. One of us. One of the good guys. A green one, sure. Maybe a little too Joe Friday. But. Always but.

My Big Chief tablet had a shopping list of loose ends and a few Manhattan rings circling in orbits of their own.

"Let's go back to Marty. Remember the lab report from the delivery truck? There were cleans on the radio where the killer apparently set it to the dance station. That doesn't fit with Moony, who was country all the way. Also, the footprints in the cemetery matched the prints from the truck. Rick says circumstantial. Then there's Moony's death. The guy's high, immersed in water, maybe a police taser can fry his circuits."

"Jack, this is sounding as thin as Rick's version."

"I know, but wait. We've got all the pieces of the porn ring except for the missing stud. Now a very scared Danswaller says I know the guy. Based on our little shootout tonight, he may have gotten himself killed over trying to tell me who. But the pictures, they're the thing."

I rummaged through my briefcase for the prints I lifted from Nancy's lab and handed them to Nash.

"See the forearms on the white guy?"

"Yeah."

"What do you see?"

"Just a guy's arm."

"Hair?"

"I don't see any. I guess he's a blonde."

"Like someone you know?"

She put the prints down and gave me the look.

"Come on, Jack. Like he's the only damn blonde on this island?"

"I know. Maybe I'm suspicious because he's standing so pat on that bogus case of his. But the night I was in the cemetery, he was taking the night off. Tonight, he's cruising on a party boat but doesn't leave a message when they land. It's little things…"

"…that start to add up, sure, but…"

"And what about that strange question: What *else* did Danswaller tell me in the graveyard? Almost like he'd heard part of it. That's been eating at me, too."

"Look, I'll grant you our Ricky has a lot to learn. That doesn't make him a killer."

"Maybe. But he's got a piece of this and I want to know what."

I readied the Bahama bed, leaving Loo the master cabin.

She sipped the last of her nudge, studying the pictures once more.

"Jack?"

"Mmm."

"You're saying Rick is this big?"

Our laughter drifted off through the mangroves.

Chapter 20
Paradise Café

"It never crossed your mind that Marshall Dillon might be gay?"

I unwrapped my legs from yet another contorted yoga position and tried to shake feeling back into my right calf.

"This is the first I've heard of it, yes."

Jonah was limber as a spring elm, moving fluidly through the class program the way an archbishop sails through the Stations of the Cross. Me, I'm the fallen man and none of this comes easily. My physical regimen, what there is left of it, consists of good old American high-impact stuff, hoops and handball, no extra points for grace. But once my drunken debt to the dexterous Mr. Lyme had exceeded my karmic credit limit, I'd reluctantly consented to join his granola-eaters every Saturday morning for an hour of mind-body-spirit connection. So far my mind was coveting my neighbor's tights, my body was creaky and uncooperative and my spirit was back on the *Jackie Oh!* Enjoying an eye-opener.

"Think about it, Jack. The whole thing with Miss Kitty? Come on. The guy can't even nail a dance hall girl who's obviously sprung on him, poor dear. They rented by the hour back then, you know. Even in black and white."

We were doing that particularly uncomfortable position that seals do so easily. I controlled the urge to bark. The pretzel girl behind me kept appraising my ass, but I couldn't tell if it was a gluteus fixation or a fashion warning. In this spandexed crowd, I looked like Scruffy the lovable mascot.

"I guess I just assumed he was above such carnal desires," I said.

"Let's see. Single, tall, gorgeous, over thirty, his best friend is a doctor. I think we know what made his gun smoke."

"I don't get cable," I said in self-defense.

Paradise Café used to be a gas station in my youth. Now the mostly conch clientele sits around waiting for their Cuban toast instead of their radiator flush, but otherwise the ambiance is about the same. I was still wiping the mind-body-spirit out of my eyes when Jonah spotted the Wilde sisters off in the corner and switched his order to go.

Towel around my neck, I carried my double OJ and café Cubano to their table. Jen looked me up and down with a coquettish grin and edged out a chair with her Rollerblade. Abby, hardly the party animal at our first meeting, didn't seem to be much of a morning person either.

"Ladies."

Jen leaned forward and gave me a playful peck at my bad ear, falling back giggling. In her sport top, bikini bottoms and in-line skates, she was a pleasantly stoned tourist attraction on wheels.

"Where'd you go last night? We missed you," she said.

"After Sloppy's, nowhere. Had a friend down from Marathon. We stayed in and talked. Work, mostly. You?"

Jen looked at her sister. "Should we tell him, Abs?"

The dour one just shrugged.

Jen leaned over and whispered, "We went clubbing with Everett. Right here in Key West."

"Clubbing? Are you nuts?"

"We all dressed as Hemingway, Jack. It was *so* fun. Ev needed it after the week he's had." She glanced at her sister. "Abs, too."

"The week he's had? How did you find him? Did he call or what?"

"He called. We met him. He had the beards and the hats, everything. Claims he got the idea from your little adventure the other night in the cemetery."

"When? When did you hook up?"

Jen looked at Abby. She just looked away.

"It must have been around midnight. Maybe a little later. We were a little toasted."

"We?" Abby asked, low simmer.

"Oh, excuse me, Sister Sourpuss, Ev and I." She leaned toward me. "Abby's taking it pretty hard."

My Cuban toast and eggs arrived. I hit the waitress up for a refill on espresso. She started to protest but I must have looked like I needed it and she walked off to shoot some steam.

"Getting a little careless for a wanted man, isn't he?"

Jen scraped her chair over next to mine.

"He wants to meet you. He couldn't last night. Tonight. After the contest."

"And my motivation would be?"

"The truth, of course. He didn't do it, Jack. This is his last chance. He can move around now at least, in disguise. After tonight, whoever's hunting him will have an easy target."

I ate my breakfast in silence, trying to sift through the new information. The waitress brought my little cup of joseppi and gave my damp hair a flick with my own towel as reprimand.

"When and where?" I asked.

"He'll find you, is all he said. He'll know where you are. At the contest, I guess. Jack, it was so fun being a man last night!" She stretched close to my ear. "I used the men's room. Standing up!"

"Mmm. That would explain the line."

Jen skated me to the door.

"You be home later?"

"I try to sleep sometime. Good practice if nothing else."

She nipped at my good ear and pressed her sport top against my soaked tee.

"Maybe I'll roll by."

"Mmm."

Nash had left for the Conch Tour Train depot by the time I returned to the *Jackie Oh!* There was a phone message from city lab. No prints on Papa's flash and battery pack. Loo might collect a few shell casings at the train yard to add to the already overflowing file marked Loose Ends, but I wasn't optimistic. The only thing I knew so far about Deadly Ernest was he didn't get by the practice range much.

I poured a cup of cold joe from the pot Nash left, grabbed a mind-body-spirit cleansing shower and pulled on my beat-up Canes gym shorts. The dull ache was history, but the stitches behind my ear were beginning to itch.

I returned to the galley just as Rick Michaels stepped aboard from his skiff. I threw open the sliding doors as he tied off.

"Swingin'."

"Tarzan."

Like I looked crazy, him in his two-tone fishing cap with the eleven-foot bills and the ear flaps. So help me, it looked like a Canadian goose had come to roost on his head.

"Good cruise last night?"

"You can laugh at Johnny all you want, he's a good guy underneath."

"I'm not laughing. He's done the time."

"Well, some people laugh."

"It's the uniform. Catches too much sunlight down here." His hat fit in there, too.

I handed Rick a can of beer and we sat outside in my weather-beaten wicker chairs beneath the shade of the top deck. The cold joe was starting to grow on me.

I went over the previous evening in detail, pausing to let the more relevant points sink into his goose-ass head. He repeated the same party line: Whoever was after Danswaller was using me to get to him. Danswaller was a fugitive in a double homicide. Who knew how many people wanted to see him dead, and maybe for very good reasons of their own? Sex. Drugs. The guy was trouble, period. He might even be trying to play me. Might have been Danswaller last night, flashing and firing, he said.

I wasn't sure how to broach the inevitable with him. While Rick made minimal attempts to disguise his sexuality, he was a private person in his professional life. No water-cooler Romeo, our Ricky. Situations like this, I guess I always jump in with two feet. They're both going to end up wet anyway.

"Look, asking around in our investigation, your name came up. With the sisters. And Marty."

He kind of winced, was all.

"It would," he sighed, looking away.

I could see shadows of deeper disappointments cross his face, the potential embarrassing moments he lived his life avoiding. He was just getting started with the business of building up barriers between his life and the world. Probably still torn over whether to do so at all. Jonah had a favorite saying: "Sidestepping other people's morality is an emotional tango. It becomes easier with age, but you're never more than one misstep away from falling on your ass."

I sipped my cold joe and watched a cormorant teach its fledgling the fine art of fishing. Sun, even nearing midday, sparkled on the water, turning the tiny ripples into a bed of diamonds on the bottle-green sea.

"You would have to have known Marty to understand, Jack. She had an appetite for living that was beyond what most people would ever dream."

"Maybe we should back up," I suggested.

He motioned. I brought him another cold one.

"I'm not very comfortable talking about this with you," he said.

"Yeah. Same here. Let's make this strictly OTR. Unless." I didn't have to spell out what unless meant.

He tipped his can and managed a constipated little smile.

"Sometime last spring, Marty and Everett and I were…" He waved, struggling for the phrase. "…an item. OK? I had just met Everett at Puss 'n' Boots. He introduced me to Marty. She liked…variety. God, this is so hard."

"Give me the condensed version."

"Marty enjoyed…doing certain things while Everett and I were…doing certain things."

"You and Marty?"

He shook his head. "She was agreeable, of course. But what's the saying?"

"Close cover before striking?"

"Funny. No. The one about the flesh being weak."

"OK, so it's you and Everett."

"Yes. And Everett and Marty."

"OK. Mixed doubles."

"So, at first it was exciting, of course. Have you ever been in a three-way, Jack?"

"This is about you, flash. Remember?"

"Yeah. Well. We were discrete. A little group-dancing at P&B, but nothing outrageous, you know. I won't do that. A few times, when Jen would ask us back to the salons, it got a little crazy perhaps. But it was never crazy enough for Marty."

"Where did Jen fit into the picture?"

"Well, Jen was like…that emperor guy, what's his name? From the porn movie."

"Caligula?" I said. From the porn movie indeed.

"That guy. She was hot for Marty, but I think she liked to watch, too. Like a ringmaster, sort of. I always figured she had a separate thing going with Marty on the side anyway. Marty spent a lot of time at that club and it wasn't always on the dance floor."

"What about the sister? Abby?"

Rick hesitated.

"She was sprung on Marty too. You could just tell. But she didn't act on it. Not that I ever saw anyway. They danced a few times maybe. She was too serious for Marty, I think. Jen and me, we could keep up with Marty in the party department. At least for a while."

"Then what?"

"Well, you've already told me most of the rest. Marty meets Moony, they start their little porn thing. The sisters want in. We kind of see the ending different, though."

"Who was the fourth? The other stud?"

"I don't know. I thought you knew."

"It wasn't you, was it?"

"Me?" Rick rose, visibly upset. "Fuck sake, Jack!"

"Forget it. I had to ask."

"Why? Why'd you have to ask?" He was getting red now.

I brought him the two photos. He glanced at them, then up at me, measuring his chances of landing a clean blow, by the looks of it.

"It's a blonde," I pointed out.

He angrily pulled out his wallet and offered me a posed portrait of himself and a sailing buddy taken prior to boarding a cruise ship. His hand was shaking in anger.

"See these arms?" He held them out. "See these? There's hair, Jack! See this photo? Hair! Blond hair!" He flipped Moony's glossies back at me in disgust. "What you've got there's a Mexican hairless freak of some kind."

He simmered as I fetched us both a fresh beer. The Germans surfaced next door, eyeing us first with curiosity, then with patronizing little we-told-you-so smirks.

"Look, Rick. On the record, I had to ask. You'd have done the same, I hope."

He looked away and sipped his beer, still seething.

I let it ride.

"What are you rigged for?" I asked at last.

"Bonefish." Petulant.

"Cooler full of these puppies, we might bring a few to Jesus."

"Yeah. Let's go."

I filled the beaten old metal box I'd inherited from Max with beers and ice. Swingin' was taking one parting look at the porn as I wedged the cooler into the bow of the skiff.

"Besides, it looks a little small to be me," he said.

"Yeah," I said. "What was I thinking?"

Chapter 21
Bonefishing

The mangroves off Halfmoon Key were well-known bonefish flats. Years ago, the charter captains informally agreed among themselves to ferry their camera-toting, catalog-shopping rod-and-reel-clubbers to specific outer islands in the interest of preserving the peaceful inner 'groves for us. There is always a balance between the commercial and the sacred in the Keys. When things swing too far to either side, things die. Like the reef. So far, we've managed to fend off the oil companies, who badly want to build their greasy little towers in these mangroves. How long that tenuous balance will last is anybody's guess.

We shut down in five feet of water on a flood tide, within easy casting distance to any number of reliable bonefish holes. I coated my shoulders and the tops of my feet with sun block and dunked my old tennis hat over the side before scrunching it down on my head. Rick took his fly gear and set up in the bow. I took the stern.

I'd ventured out for bone a couple times since M., but it was never the same for me. Some guys like fishing with the guys. Better than fishing alone, they say, or worse, with the wife. Me, I liked fishing with M. Truth is, my real second choice is not fishing at all.

The call came in from her boss one blazing-hot morning. I'd just returned to my fifth-floor downtown office from a standing three-on-three game some of the guys at Metro-Dade had put together to battle the winter bulge, which down here comes in the summer. He wanted to personally invite me to a working lunch at Bayside, where Pete had agreed to at least listen to what he and his federal brethren had cooked up this time. I gave a quick call to M. Information was sketchy but she was liking the sound of it. She'd been on a tear about secretary spread since being reassigned to drug surveillance. I couldn't see it myself. But then I couldn't see a lot of things.

I walked in and sweated over Pete's desk until he'd had enough and ditched his phone call. Yes, the feds had a match made in heaven for a young couple with the experience and the guts to see it through. Yes, based on what little he actually knew about it, there would be promo points involved, meaning career advancement. And yes, I was an awful pain in his ass, and proceeded to list the reasons why, starting with the little cesspool I'd made of his inbox.

I got approximately zip done all morning, savoring the prospect of finally working with M. She hadn't been able to talk, of course, it being the bureau and all, but I could hear in her voice that extra breath between sentences that said she shared my excitement. We'd laughed about it so many times. The A Team, we'd called ourselves. If they'd only throw one to the A Team. To think they were actually doing just that. Undercover together. It was all just too *too*.

The script was a career-maker, anybody could see that. The young scion of a Midwest cattle fortune and his new bride move into a mansion on Biscayne Bay, looking to combine his interest in the film industry with her taste for the nightlife. Hubby logs long hours schmoozing with producers, directors, actresses and assorted cling-ons, learning the buzzwords of the trade, a mover and shaker in training. Meanwhile, his young ladylove indulges in indulgence, spending with abandon, allowing herself to be enticed up the wicked, wicked recreational drug food chain until she is clubbing with the top players in the Miami cartel.

That was step one. It took about two months to connect with our new friends. Armed with tens of thousands of disposable taxpayer dollars, I wrestled the seduction of power while M. struggled with a rush of a different sort, one with which I was all too recently familiar. We talked each other through it as best we could. It would be all right, we told each other, maybe even believing it a little.

Still, undercover, paranoia erases the lines you're normally used to living within and replaces them with situations. Everything becomes dictated by the situation, from the shoes you wear to the wine you order to the fellows you end up letting the air out of. In the end, if you survive, you're left to deal with the moral issues. That can be every bit as harrowing as coming off smack. Some don't make it.

Step two required great finesse on our part to sink the hook. The script finds hubby's film in financial trouble and his fortunes dwindling. Hubby and wife are drifting apart. Wife, at the end of her rope, asks her cartel friends if they know of a way for hubby to make a quick several mil to bail out his movie. And of course they do.

Gradually, we began to mingle our business and social circles, not a difficult feat on the face of it, but ever so delicate because of the widespread paranoia within both the drug and film worlds. Moreover, it was imperative that certain players meet certain players in a logical order, at particular times, under exact conditions, to move the plot along. At this stage, one minor slip could take weeks to recoup; a major blunder could be fatal, literally. Show too much interest, or too little, at the wrong time and we'd be left to explain our rather elaborate spending spree to Uncle Sam. And that was the best-case scenario. More likely, guys who make their living in personnel disposal would arrive unannounced with our free one-way tickets to the continental shelf.

M. was expert at the subtleties of it all, cajoling, advising, pleading, flirting, commiserating, complimenting and gently chastising each of the players into position with the skill of a Grand Master. She gave so much of herself to her part that I felt unworthy to share the same stage. Had my role been written cagey instead of thick as a mud fence, my inferior performance surely would have been apparent to this bunch. As it was, I was quite convincing as the half-wit son of a bundle whose all-thumbs business sense made him the quintessential mark.

We'd been undercover nearly five months by Thanksgiving, which we spent in the Carolinas debriefing with Pete and the FBI tact team. M. was holding, of course. Who wouldn't be, tucked that far up in the Smokeys? Moonshine's not going to put out this fire, Pa. Likely the feds knew, but it never came up. King's X, I guess. We had rather awkward meals in a meeting room off the main lodge, our bosses and fellow cops trying to reach us, M. and me pretending to be reachable. We weren't. Not by then.

At night, she would sit in the dark in the kitchen of our tiny cabin and smoke cigarettes and cry. Sometimes I would pull up a vinyl-covered tubular chair and sit beside her, stroking her hair, wracking my brain for words to calm her. I could feel her teeth clench from the back of her head. She wore no makeup the entire four days. She may have bathed once. We held each other, or tried to, but it was strange and tentative, the way you might touch the victim, coming upon a car wreck. We had lost whatever makes people want to make love.

Over pecan pie and joe by the gallon, we and the buzzcuts scripted the third and final act. If everything went well, they said, we'd be back home in the Grove by Christmas. Once we'd returned to our luxurious foxhole to play out the final scene, that became our litany: Home in the Grove by Christmas, home in the Grove by Christmas…

Swingin' Dick stopped suddenly in mid-reel.

"Jack…"

I turned. A half-mile off and closing, a deep red cigarette boat was making directly for us at a speed and attitude you didn't see in Halfmoon Key, ever.

"You expecting company?" I asked.

Rick shook his head. We both reeled like mad.

"What do you have with you?"

"Flare gun. You?"

"A half-rack of cold cans and a Louisville Slugger Junior. Radio?"

He shook his head no.

We quickly stowed the rods and fired up the little outboard. It was more than a trawler but no match for the twin diesels heading our way. Still, maneuvering power in tight quarters was something the big speedboat would give up to us, especially if we could run deeper into the mangroves before all those seahorses arrived.

Rick pulled the hook. I kicked the skiff into high gear.

"I hope this guy drives as well as he shoots," I said.

I sprinted between two sizable mangrove islands, keeping one eye to our back while Rick tended to the depth. I'd fished these maze-like channels years before, but like the Keys themselves, they were ever changing and I knew my memory chart would be useless. I quickly determined the nearest narrow passage and headed for it at full bore. We arrived at its mouth a split second late as the cigarette boat came slithering through the mangrove break, hot on our wake. The only surprises left now were ahead of us.

Rick unpacked the flare gun from beneath the center console and field-checked it before loading. I had no idea of the range or accuracy of the thing, but it didn't much matter; Plan B would be pitching cold beer cans from ten yards, Plan C wasn't really worth thinking about.

"What're we drawing now?" I yelled.

Rick squinted into the sun-dappled water rushing beneath the bow. "About a fathom!"

My height. Way too deep.

He scrambled back to the stern, tucking the flare gun into the waist of his shorts. "I can see the beard now. And the hat."

I slalomed the skiff through a couple tight spots, sending the little outboard motor bouncing off a mangrove root here and there. If I could keep the screw free and in one piece, we might stand a chance of slipping this pirate. Or given enough time, we might get lucky and lure him aground, if we could find any ourselves. Distance was our only ally. We were in no position to come out on the happy end of a show of arms.

I dodged and weaved ever eastward toward Halfmoon Key proper in hopes of putting a hidden shoal between us. The tightening web of mangrove forests and blind rivers would slow him down some, but the green Gulf water beneath us remained annoyingly navigable. Rick's worried looks from the bow only confirmed my hunch that nature was not going to run the kind of interference we needed to stop a half-ton death boat.

The roar of the twin diesels grew louder, closing on us. As I pressed through a break in the foliage, my stomach dropped. We had run out of mangrove and suddenly found ourselves delivered back into open water, an unreachable distance from the next sanctuary.

Someone, in less dire circumstances no doubt, once said that life consists of what you do with plan B. If so, we were about to do some serious living.

Several silent rounds hissed into the wake behind us.

"Where do you want to die, Swingin', sun or shade?" I wasn't sure I was kidding.

"We might maneuver better in open water, you think?" Rick's voice was shaky as a blind date.

"Get the anchor coiled and make sure it's cleated. We get a chance, we might use it. Also, bring me the tender.

That way I'll know when we get within a ten-foot pole of Papa."

I smiled. He tried. The kid was OK.

I flattened the throttle down full and set a course straight out to sea.

The twin diesels sounded like approaching thunder over my shoulder. Rick crouched at the bow, frantically coiling anchor line. The bad news was, we couldn't outrun or outmaneuver the speedboat at full throttle in open water. The good news, if you could call it that, was that Papa would have a tough time running us down and capsizing the skiff while pursuing us. Still, there was that nagging matter of the silent gun.

I altered our course by forty-five degrees every fifteen seconds or so to buy as much time as possible. Stealing glances aft, I recognized the khaki cap and unkempt white hair behind the tinted windshield. Silent gunfire was beginning to ricochet around the fiberglass skiff as the distance between us narrowed.

"The cooler!" I yelled, pointing. Rick brought it aft.

I stood up, fastened the latch securely, and stationed the old girl on end in the captain's seat, beer, ice and Max's metal box guarding my back. I motioned for Rick to take cover behind the center console.

The deep red speedboat advanced off our starboard side, the earsplitting roar of its engines all but drowning the high-pitched protest of our little outboard. Shots caromed off the rails. I tensed, waiting for the penetration, followed by the numbness, then the burning. Two rounds made hollow thuds through the captain's chair and into Max's cooler but failed to reach me. My angle of protection was fast disappearing as the bloody red bow entered into my peripheral vision.

"Hold on!" I warned Rick.

As the red bow came even with me, I yanked the throttle back suddenly, from full to idle, sending the sleek, deadly racer speeding on by, and bucking us violently, in his wake as well as our own backwash.

The death boat bobbed, sputtering and spewing, awash in its power water. Then its terrible bow lurched upward as the red hull heeled in a high-powered turn.

I kicked the skiff into full throttle. Its single screw dug deep into the green water, lifting us up at a dangerous pitch. We hadn't even reached a plane by the time we were upon and past the departing bow of the racer, which corkscrewed in an awkward attempt to lock in on our new position. Several shots rang off the skiff.

I cut the engine again. We settled. The red boat was off to port now, completing a tight loop for an approach at us broadside. I reversed the engine and turned, facing Papa bow to bow.

"Rick, get the anchor ready! We've only got one shot at the cockpit!"

I punched it. Like some open-water version of Chicken, I barreled head-on toward a craft twice our size traveling at twice our speed. I only hoped I wouldn't run out of nerve before I ran out of water.

The shots came straight at us this time, glancing off the console, shattering the windshield. I watched through the spokes of the upper wheel as the red monster approached, growing larger by the second. The killer fully intended to crush us, there was no question about that. The few feints I made were answered in kind. His speed and deadly bearing only increased as the distance between us hissed away.

I kept the throttle full out, something I'd learned on the gridiron several lives ago. Hit them harder and it doesn't hurt as much. At least that's the theory.

Looking down the long, sleek barrel of that red bow, a split second away from all the water I could ever drink, I held my breath and went hard to port, the unnatural or crazy direction, like turning into the oncoming lane in traffic. Several things happened in rapid succession: Rick rose from a crouch to launch the anchor in a high arc toward the tinted windshield of the cigarette boat, I was thrown like a rag doll against the port rail from the force of the oncoming wake, and our motor stalled in the tumultuous wash.

Blood poured into my left eye, suddenly swollen nearly shut from the impact. I struggled to my feet. The skiff had taken on a half-foot of water but we were afloat, barely.

I scrambled to Rick, spread-eagled at the bow, thrown half overboard, the water running red beneath him. Carefully, I lifted and turned his body. His face had gone putty-white. He was shot above the knee, possibly twice, but he was alive.

I grabbed my floating tee shirt, wrapped it tight around the source of most of the blood, and secured it with fish line I bit free from the rod. Sloshing back to the cooler, I stripped off my outriggers, scooped up a half-dozen cold beers and what little ice remained, and jury-rigged an ice pack to slow the flow of blood to his leg.

Before I could apply the cold pack, he stopped me, reached inside the bag of beers and took one, holding it out to me. I lifted the tab for him.

"You manage this?" I asked him.

He finished his long draw. "Yeah," he said, clearly unsure.

I had bigger problems.

"Jack?" It was almost a whisper.

"Yeah?"

"His aim's getting better," he said.

Then he passed out.

The skiff was a bathtub half-filled with murky pink water. I gave the outboard a couple bulb-pumps of fuel and tried to fire it. Nothing.

The deadly red cigarette boat was circling wide off to our port side, preparing to finish the job. I watched it for several seconds. There was a flaw in its wake I couldn't explain at first, then it dawned on me: it was the anchor line. Rick's toss had landed somewhere on the boat. I checked the cleat. We were still tethered. The line was active, turning with the arc of the race boat, not yet taut but getting there.

I didn't have much time. Quickly, I hauled the anchor line in and made a couple loops around the center console, then uncleated and tied the end off on the line itself. When the slack ran out, we would now stand an even chance of being towed, rather abruptly, instead of merely popping the cleat. I wasn't sure I wanted to be tied to Papa's torpedo boat, but it carried more survival possibilities than sitting dead in the water.

I traced the path of the anchor line and braced against Rick for liftoff. When it came, the death knell of the twin diesels suddenly deepened and the skiff lurched backward, digging awkwardly into the water. The line snapped to and shook the daylights out of the center console. The remaining flotsam in our little blood bath, including Max's cooler and our fishing gear, swept overboard as if expelled by a sneeze. As our speed and drag increased, the skiff came about, correcting violently to a bow-forward plane, the anchor line singing like a piano string above our heads.

We skimmed that way for a short time before Papa realized what had happened and cut his engines. We drifted ahead from inertia, a situation I recognized as endangering our toehold on the red boat. I leapt to the bow and began hauling the slack in and wrapping it around the console. It wasn't much, I knew. Papa could be tossing the anchor overboard or cutting the line while I was struggling to keep from giving him enough slack to yank the skiff apart. But what if he wasn't, or couldn't?

He started up again, slower this time, and steadily built to a dangerous speed. My fears of being yanked off the planet were quickly replaced by new ones as the red boat headed directly toward a string of mangroves. As we closed in on the thick growth, Papa took a wide arc familiar to water skiers as the prelude to 'crack the whip'. There was little doubt just where Papa planned to deposit us.

I rummaged through the pockets of my outriggers for my fish knife and began sawing at the anchor line as the mangroves loomed off the bow. He had already made the snapping part of the turn that could catapult us into oblivion.

Ten yards from shore the line snapped like a gunshot. I threw my weight against the starboard rail in hopes of digging in broadside and slowing our deathblow. It worked. The skiff bounced hard against the mangrove roots and back out into open water.

The red boat slowly turned again for blood. I saw the wake kick up behind the speedboat. It would be on us in less than a minute. I tried the outboard one last time. No go.

Rick looked like a broken toy, misshapen, discarded. Then I spotted the flare gun handle sticking out from the waist of his blood-soaked shorts. I climbed over and grabbed it, checking the chamber. We had two rounds, if they fired.

The red boat roared directly toward us. I took position behind the center console and prepared for the showdown. As the race boat got closer, I saw the windshield had been shattered and partly torn away by the blow from the anchor. There were bloody red traces around the white hair and beard of the driver, whisking back from what looked at this distance like dark glasses. Swingin' had scored a few points there, all right.

I let the hurtling missile close to within five yards before I stood up and fired the flare. I saw it enter into the cockpit, then everything disappeared in an explosion of salt spray.

The impact of the rushing wake nearly foundered our battered skiff, which seemed to have developed a life and a will of its own to survive. I heard the thud as Rick was tossed from rail to rail, beer cans flying free. I clung to the wheel with one hand, the other gripped tight to the flare gun, and was nearly swept overboard by the eruption of water.

The spray seemed to fall forever. There were noises I wasn't sure I'd heard, so certain was I that we would surely be crushed by the craft. Then, oddly, I smelled smoke.

I crept to my knees and peered out. Ten yards off, in the very mangroves we'd just bounced off, sat the wreckage of the red speedboat, smoking and spewing, its monster twin diesels dead at last.

I waited several minutes for human response from the wreck while I righted Rick and reset his leg wrapping. Then I slipped over the side—not much of a slip at that point—and swam the skiff to the red boat. I read the bow: *Surprise*, out of Key Weird.

I climbed a tangle of mangrove roots to board the sleek machine, holding the flare gun ridiculously like some JIC .45. But there were only mechanical noises left on board.

The flare had apparently thrown the driver violently to the rear of the cockpit, then the impact with the mangrove had tossed him back against the front of the cockpit. I approached the body cautiously, kicking it with my bare foot a couple times before kneeling down for a closer look. The hat and white wig were long gone. The charred beard was down around his neck like a noose.

I turned him over.

Eyes wide open, teeth bared in a death grimace, the last seconds of Everett Danswaller's life had clearly been horrific.

As I looked into his frozen features, some of the flesh at the back of my neck went cold. There would be no more cat-and-mouse in the dark, no more cemeteries and kiddie-train yards. Only thee and me, dear Papa, and an island scarcely big enough for both of us.

Returning to the skiff, I fished around in the thinning blood for the last beer on board and popped it. Collapsing back next to Rick, I took a long draw and fired the last flare into the clear blue sky.

Chapter 22
The Parting

I managed to make quick work of the Coast Guard, considering. They had a carrier full of questions and I had a dinghy full of answers, sitting there in my skivvies with the biggest shiner of my life, smoking a bummed cigarette. But once I convinced them to radio and confirm that we were indeed cops, things took more of a jeezus-you're-two-lucky-dicks tone.

Rick came to as the air-evac chopper arrived.

"All the beer's gone," I informed him.

"How'd it turn out?" he asked.

I offered the short version: "We're alive. Danswaller's dead."

Rick winced, getting that deep burning now. "Case closed then," he said with effort. "Maybe he was…flash boy after all."

"Yeah. Maybe," I said, though I knew better.

They strapped him onto the stretcher, inserted an IV in his left forearm and clipped a blood pressure monitor to his earlobe. Then he was gone in a saltwater froth. I tossed my butt into the rotor wash.

The craggy-faced old CO of the patrol boat wasn't happy about the shellac job I was feeding him and told me so in the colorful language of his people. Too much damage of a suspicious nature to the little skiff for his taste, apparently. I sank into the otherworldly pleasures of a government-issue ice pack and offered mumbles and shrugs. Against his better judgment, he said, but as a professional courtesy, blah blah blah, he reluctantly agreed to deliver me back to the *Jackie Oh!*

I poured a full fist of bourbon, lit one from my own pack and stood in my briefs in front of the wheezy old window unit, set permanently to max cold, knob broken off. They'd be shoring up the plumbing in Rick's left leg about now. That was a first for the kid, you could tell. Always that look of surprise that it doesn't hurt worse. And then it does.

Excluding my recent face tuck, I hadn't been shot since that cold December day when M. drew her get-out-of-reality-free card and took leave of all this.

Our fast new friends, primarily Hollywood demagogues, narcissistic Eurotrash and pidgin-speaking cartel middlemen, were quick to rally around if it looked like there might be something in it for them. And of course we went to great lengths to make it always appear that there was. Success gives off the scent of fear. Our new crowd was our new crowd precisely because they smelled it.

M. had become wafer-thin from the flake and the life. So much for secretary spread. Conversations that had once lasted for hours now dragged on for minutes. We ate in silence when we ate together. The case itself, once our dream, had almost ceased to matter, as if it were now one of our what-if scenarios and the artificial life was what was real.

We'd been back in town a couple weeks from our Smoky Mountain getaway when all the stars aligned. A million-six in uncut Columbian blow would be ours to retail as we pleased, using freelance or cartel operatives. Cash buy, net somewhere in the twenties. Keep the cameras rolling, keep the fictitious investors happy, keep the mirror ball spinning. Right from the script, pulling everybody's houses down with it. M. and me, home in the Grove by Christmas, music up, fade to credits.

The morning sky was low and gray as we drove north to Lauderdale. At Bahia Mar marina, we joined the four cartel boys aboard the *Noisette*, BVI registry, and set out for some offshore privacy. Drinks, flake and catered crudité to a Latin disco beat. If they had metal detectors, they didn't use them. Hand it to M., she'd done a great job gaining their trust.

We discussed the usual inane things: Could I get someone's daughter a speaking part? Were we going to Cannes? What about a location shoot in Cali? With enough money, I said, all things are possible. M. laughed at that, perfectly in character. It was the last time I would ever hear her laugh.

When we reached the edge of the Atlantic shelf where the water turns a deep electric blue, the businessmen instructed the captain to shut down all engines. There was barely a swell on that gray winter day. We could have still been dockside at Bahia Mar for the motion of the sea beneath us.

The two assistants cleared away the hors d'oeuvres from the meeting table and we seated ourselves, M. to my right, facing our two Latin friends. I noticed her chair angled slightly away from mine but thought nothing of it. We'd hit a little rough patch. You get on each other's nerves now and then, more so undercover. We'd learned a lot together in this. It was all about to be worth it. It was all about to be over. Home in the Grove by Christmas.

The older of the two businessmen motioned to an aide, who brought a small aluminum case forward and placed it on the table. The younger of the two businessmen nodded for me to open it. I did. Inside was the coke, vacuum sealed in five-kilo bags. I picked one up and held it. Then I smiled and nodded like a new father.

M. leaned over and touched my arm. I lifted my carry-on bag to the table, turned the handle away from me and slid it over to the two. The older one smiled contentedly while the younger one sprang the latches and peered at the stacks and stacks of crisp Benjamins. Then he picked up a packet, rifled to the middle of it and shined a laser penlight through a bill. Then Ir. Then he placed the money back in the case.

"This money is marked," the young one said.

"That's ridiculous," I said, remaining seated.

M. looked away.

The young one rose, closed the carry-on and turned the handle back toward me.

"We have enjoyed your company," he said in closing.

With that, the two young bucks behind us advanced. I grabbed the cash bag and rotated in my chair, bringing the hard corner of the case into one tough's jewels. He crumpled. I stood and drew my .45 on the other. He froze momentarily, then relaxed, grinning at what he saw over my shoulder. I cautiously turned.

The young businessman held M., a knife to her throat.

I stepped sideways to get an aim at both of them. "Let her go," I said.

"I'm afraid this is not your movie, Mr. Jack." His blade produced a drop of blood, the promise of more to follow. "Eduardo."

Goon number two took my gun and the bag of money.

"Let's get some air now, shall we?" the young one said.

The older businessman retired to the bar and poured himself a drink. The younger one ushered M. out of the cabin. The goons shoved me along behind.

They herded us to the bow, where a teakwood bridge extended a half-dozen feet beyond the hull.

"Put him there! *Andale!*" the young boss ordered. His henchmen pushed me out onto the narrow plank. A chrome rail was all that separated me from the big blue below.

He handed M. off to the other goon and began to pace back and forth, enjoying the metronome click of his hard leather heels as he appraised me in my little cage.

"You are no doubt a *federale*, Mr. Jack. Whether your lovely companion and our dear friend is also, I do not know. But she has helped us so far."

I looked at M., searching. She looked away. He looked at M. She gave him just the right look, a mix of confusion, hurt and fear. Vulnerable. Sexy, even. It would have been a take in my movie.

"This is a simple question of loyalty, is it not, Mr. Jack?" he continued, pacing. "Loyalty to your friends, the ones who would help you when you need it, mmm?"

"Let her go," I said. "She doesn't have anything to do with this." I could practically hear the words land cold at my feet like hailstones.

"Perhaps it is as you say," he said, stroking his goatee. "Perhaps you have deceived her and used her as well as us, yes?"

I didn't reply.

M. braced against her captor's pistol.

The boss paced some more, lost in contemplation. At last, he stopped.

"I can't be sure. You can see that, can't you, Jack? I mean, you are expendable. But my dear friend will have to convince me with a simple favor. A test. A test of loyalty. Bring her!"

The goon shoved M. toward the bow. The young businessman produced a gold cigarette case and lit one up, then mindful of his manners, motioned the case toward me. I nodded. He handed off a lit cigarette to the recovering goon, who carefully offered it to me. We smoked a minute. I glanced up at the pilothouse. The captain and mate were keeping their eyes far, far out to sea.

The young businessman finally flicked his smoke overboard and walked over to M. Reaching into his suit coat, he pulled out a handgun. I braced.

"You see, my dear, Mr. Jack is already dead. You must not think of it as killing him. You must think of it as a favor. A favor to me, yes?"

He handed M. the gun and held his arm toward me, presenting her with the opportunity.

"Please. *Por favor.*"

M. raised the gun slowly, holding it straight-arm, as if she'd never fired one. Her eyes were miles away as they rose to meet mine. I reached in, hoping to find her. Braced against the rail, I searched for any hint of a future, for me, for us. Home in the Grove by Christmas, I thought. Real hard.

Staring into her eyes down the barrel of a gun for the second time in our lives, I suddenly felt less sure of the outcome. Was the heady combination of the flake and the life too enticing to just walk away from? We'd drifted these months. We both thought we were prepared for it, but you never really are. Situations again, sewing doubts.

I saw her hand tighten in the grip. Then, without hesitation, she turned and fired. The young man dropped, the right side of his head gone.

I ducked and ran without thinking toward her. She spun on the first goon and shot him in the chest, the explosion sending him staggering backward, overboard.

The second goon fired.

I reached M. at the very moment the bullet did.

I pulled her behind me and freed the gun from her wilting hand. A second round hit me in the flank and a third caught my left arm above the elbow as I rolled.

I dropped the advancing goon with a head shot from five feet that scattered the remainder of his thoughts onto the pilothouse windows above. The mate hastily bolted the door as the captain started the engines.

I fell to my knees over M. and lifted her into my arms. There was too much blood, we both knew it.

I held her to me, feeling the last beats of her heart flow into mine.

Then she was gone.

I staggered to the salon. The old man looked up surprised from his drink. I hit him beside the head with the flat of the pistol, hard enough to knock him out.

Then I poured myself one and waited for the cavalry.

Chapter 23
Surprise

I felt the wheels descend the wooden ramp to the *Jackie Oh!* I pulled open the front door. Jen fell sobbing into my arms.

"Everett…" she sputtered, mascara I didn't know she had flowing freely down her reddened cheeks.

"You heard?"

"They…called…Althea."

Sure. Coast Guard. Next of kin.

I lifted her inside and kicked the door closed.

She clung to my neck, wheels slipping out from under her. I absorbed her staccato tremors and managed to get a few gulps from my drink down her before the quaking sobs started all over again. I steered her against the wall for stability until she gained control.

"I…came…right…over," she said. One good look at my face, she pushed me away suddenly. "Jack, what…?"

"I was there, Jen."

"When Ev—?" She stood back against the wall, taking in my bloody briefs and the bruises. "Oh my God!"

"Rick's shot up pretty bad."

"Shot? But Ev…" She welled up again. "Abby told me he was going fishing."

"Mmm. *Surprise* your boat?"

She nodded, tears breaking. She took my drink in both hands as instructed and drank what was left.

"I'd call your insurance agent."

I lit her one of mine and traded it for her empty glass, then poured us each another. She rolled to the window AC unit and draped her tanned arms over her head, taking in the cool full on her tube top, smoking defiantly in the icy breeze. I stood in the kitchen, watching her from behind.

"Serves Ricky right," she decided.

I wasn't inclined to debate the matter. Besides, it probably did.

"Ev didn't do it."

I agreed with that, too.

"I wish I'd never met the little bitch." Her voice shaky now.

I sat on the barstool. "All roads lead back to Marty," I said.

She turned toward me. "Meaning what?" A sudden edge there.

I just smoked.

"Because if you're implying that I had anything to do with…" and the tears started up again.

I brought her a tumbler of courage and held her, feeling the warmth of the day still resident in her taut, tender flesh. She collected herself in time and took a sip, glaring at me with a hurt, pouting expression.

"Let's talk about the boat," I suggested.

"Abby called. She lets Ev use it from time to time."

"When did she call?"

"I don't know. When I got home. Noon, maybe."

"You two own the boat?"

She shook her head. "Our family. Daddy uses it when he comes down, since he and mother split. A real bimbo magnet."

"Does he come down often?"

She frowned. "Too often."

"Abby keeps the keys then?"

Jen shrugged. "She runs the business."

Her knee rubbed up the inside of my leg as her free hand slipped beneath the waistband of my briefs, round back.

"When I heard the news, all I could think of was I wanted to be with you," she said, putting her cheek to my chest. "Just you, holding me. I didn't know about any of this."

Part of me wanted to believe her.

I repeated the litany for her sake. "Marty had a little enterprise with Moony, Danswaller and a third guy. Three of the four are dead, maybe all of them by now. You and Marty were seen clubbing with Rick, now he's shot up. Rick says he didn't pose for pesos, so the question is, who did?"

"I told you, Jack, I don't know. I don't want to know. Not about that."

"You were paying him."

"Abby was, yes. It was business. You know everything. We talked about that."

"Let's talk about Abby. She had a crush on Marty too."

Jen sighed and coasted to the barstool, helping herself to my pack.

"Everybody had a crush on Marty, Jack," she said, lighting up. "Don't you get it? She was up to it. She could just...go. You know?"

"Did you have sex with Everett?"

Jen looked away, consumed in smoke.

"Moony?"

Her eyes flared. "Jealousy, Jack? I didn't expect that from you."

I shook my head. "Curiosity. Just trying to find out who didn't get their piece of the pie and was willing to kill for it."

"Everybody got their piece of the pie, Jack, believe me. Everybody."

"Then somebody wanted more."

She laughed bitterly. "Yeah, somebody did," she agreed.

I looked questioningly at her. "Mind telling me who?"

"Marty, of course. There was never enough for Marty."

I could feel at that moment M. smiling down as the tumblers rolled into place and the combination to the puzzle revealed itself to me.

Jen washed me up and gave my battered body a thorough physical, a couple of times, neither of us thinking to remove her blades. I eventually lost consciousness and woke up alone, the sun on the far side of the island.

I called on the kid, first off. He was out of the woods and heavily medicated. I brewed some joe and listened to my answer machine. Jonah logged in with breakfast coordinates, the Tallahassee twins recited their final evening's itinerary in the most enticing tones, and Nash called, hours ago now, to say she was going to look up the Wilde sisters on a hunch. The Coast Guard must have swallowed my story for now, since there were no messages to field from my reporter friends.

In my shaving mirror, my eye looked slightly better, discoloration up, swelling down. I lifted my earlobe where a few stitches had torn loose. Rough week for the old port side. I rummaged around until I found my orange prescription vial, tapped the last two C3s into my palm and gunned them with the watered-down remains of somebody's drink.

About the last place in this world I wanted to be after M. left my side for good was front and center at her funeral. I was already well into an alcohol sprint in hopes of catching up with her and my interest in the details of earthly living was fast fading into the distance. Her boss, her family and Pete somehow talked some sense into me. We were heroes, they said. Highest honors. That was our consolation prize, I thought. Inside, I was ashamed, bone-achingly ashamed of myself. For everything, of course, but most particularly for surviving. There's nothing like surviving the one you love to really blow out your pilot light.

The department required me to take two weeks paid leave following our half-year undercover. Counseling, too; in my case, grief counseling, in addition to the usual head-shrinking, ear-bashing stiffer-upper stuff. I was not sober. I did not hear or care. I was living with M. in the Grove, home in the Grove by Christmas, home on the bloody range of my mind. Even M. told me things in those early days, encouraging things, which I took to be hallucinations triggered by the rash of great advice I was so dutifully ignoring. I paid heed to none of it.

Once back on the job, of course, there were consequences and repercussions. An unstable cop is a liability. Pete could have easily washed his hands of me to great applause all around. More than a few of the suits upstairs still considered me an irresponsible coke fag. Pete pinning a medal on my chest rankled them all the more. Me smelling like a distillery at squad meetings just rubbed their noses in it.

I was delivered from my own demise by Pete's sudden departure to these Elysian fields. I was far beyond caring where I worked, or even if, at that point. I was busy measuring myself for a casket when Pete decided there was something worth salvaging in the third drunk from the end of the bar. Maybe that appealed to the scavenger in me. My people have always been adept at pulling something of value from the sea, turning loss to profit. I wasn't convinced there was enough left to salvage in my case, but I took his offer just to get the hell out of the Grove, where the pain was becoming too keen.

Home in the Grove by Christmas turned into home to the Keys to die. I didn't think I would live long enough for my medical coverage to kick in, so I didn't sign up for any. I never pumped more than five bucks in gas. I let the Jeep's tags expire. I wouldn't even buy green bananas. I was ready to upload this sorry human file but I could never seem to get online.

Until Papa.

Papa's got the goods to do 'er, mano a mano, the honorable way. Send me off the planet and end this suffering. There are people who care about me, Jonah says. The catch is, I'm not one of them. He's bound and determined I'll get over that, I'll live through this and embrace puppies and sunsets and the holy *New York Times* crossword puzzle, and then I'll be damn glad I held on. Me, it still seems like a long shot. It would be the height of irony to be dispatched by such a lousy marksman now that I had the case practically solved.

I made a quick phoner to the Garrison Bight harbormaster. We had a friendly little chat regarding the comings and goings aboard the good ship *Surprise* that confirmed what I'd already pieced together. Then I scribbled Nash a brief itinerary, dictated the same info into her voice mail, and drove my aching body to Yo Sake.

Jonah had a serious kimono thing going lately, though he was in denial, as usual. I had my own theory regarding his sudden Orient-ation: it provided an acceptably *haute couture* way to revive his prized feather-cut wigs from the Eighties without appearing glam-rock, a style he now loathes. It also gave his feet a break from the rigors of his job.

Whatever the case, it wasn't hard to spot the gai-gin geisha with the crossword at the sushi bar.

He looked up and winced. I guess I'd grown used to it.

"The case is moving along, I see."

I sat carefully. What few bodily parts Everett Danswaller had managed to miss had been summarily punished by my insatiable roller girl. Even the C3s seem to have given up on me.

I ordered a bourbon, beer back.

"Have you narrowed the field down, or is most of the island still suspect?" Jonah, talking to his puzzle.

"Your favorite kid detective and I were nearly killed by Danswaller off Halfmoon Key today. Rick's going to live but the Bahamian's gone."

"I thought he wasn't your man?"

"Isn't. Wasn't."

"Mr. Michaels is enjoying his victory, no doubt."

"No doubt."

"So who's Papa?"

My sedatives arrived. I kicked the shot back and sipped the head off the beer.

"I've got it down to a couple candidates. Danswaller used the sisters' boat."

"The Wilde girls? Jack, you don't think…"

"One, the sisters haven't even been threatened by Papa. I find that strange. Two, Jen said something today, that Marty wanted more than she was getting. The only place she could have gotten more was from her employers, the sisters again. Third, the harbormaster at the Bight says he saw two males, one black, one white, preparing the sisters' cigarette boat late morning."

"I know, this one's got a few loose ends of its own. I mean, if it's one of the sisters, who screwed the little cowgirl's head and why? And how does the mystery boy-toy fit into all this? Was that him with Danswaller at the dock today? I don't know. But it makes more sense than Rick's version. Danswaller was living large off Marty, why would he kill the goose? He had no reason to kill Moony either, they were partners. The sisters, well, there's another story. My gut says something went south with the porno and heads started to roll."

"So to speak," he said with the look.

"So to speak." It hurt to grin.

Jonah selected a few raw fish creations. I ordered the flaming pu-pu platter. I always address sushi by its

Christian name: bait. Doesn't make any friends at a sushi bar though.

"So you're suggesting one of the sisters dressed like Papa and chased you around the rock?"

"That's where the evidence is taking me, yes. I know it sounds farfetched."

He folded his puzzle away and looked at me, sipping his sake thoughtfully.

"Jen, maybe," he said. "The other one, I don't know. Even disguised, that seems like a stretch. At least Jen's athletic enough. But I dare say I don't have to tell you that."

Jonah popped a baitball into his mouth, made an eye-roll to heaven and motioned with his chopsticks for me to try one. I saluted his offer with my beer. Call it what you will, bait is bait.

"Jen claims she's come clean," I said. "And everything she's said checks out. But there's still something troubling me about her."

"Not that little lesbian issue, I hope."

"I'm more concerned with the little liar issue. I don't know how far I can trust her, as plausible as her story sounds."

I worked my way around my little flaming sacrifice to the fish gods, to the delight of exactly none of my cosmopolitan bar mates. The shots and beers seemed to offend them, too. Delicate crowd, this bunch. I didn't have the heart to tell them what was really under Jonah's kimono.

The Hemingway Days Parade was about to begin down Duval. I gave Jonah a lift to the club through the backstreets.

"Jack, seriously, be careful tonight," Jonah said. "As you say, you're it now, and this could be their last chance. At least have the decency to not go all male on me, OK?"

I lit a smoke.

"Anything happens, I want you to have my frequent flier miles."

Chapter 24
Papa

I was feeling an uneasy breeze on my backside as I wedged my way toward my esteemed colleagues at the judge's table, ringside at Sloppy's. The town was already in its cups and still no sign of Nash. Calls to her machine and mine had proven useless. The sisters Wilde hadn't picked up either. I checked with Pete, family man at home on a Saturday night. He hadn't heard from her and offered to drive down and cover my back. Hold off, I told him, she'll turn up.

The title bout of the look-alike contest cranked up the craziness several notches. The spectators were even more unruly, if that were possible, this being the last night in town for most of them. The finalists primped and redoubled their efforts to attain ultimate Papa-ness while the also-rans kicked beers back faster than the old man himself. The judges, glazed over from the drunken semis, just wanted to survive the thing. In short, it was a typical Key Weird event, awash in its own wretched excess.

The ubiquitous Hemingway beard and frosty mane had taken on a nightmarish quality for me over the course of the week, from the old fisherman's description of the last minutes of Marty Orleans' young life to the lifeless horror-mask of Everett Danswaller, blown free from his disguise by forces he could neither fully understand nor control. I didn't think I would be judging next year's contest, even if I lived that long.

The crowd erupted in drunken cheers as a Papa finalist stripped off his jungle-cruise outerwear to reveal a feminine wardrobe underneath. It wasn't pretty, considering his girth, but it did bring to mind my breakthrough in the case. Could I imagine either of the Wilde sisters, disguised as America's heavyweight literary champ, actually pursuing me with a weapon? Or had this case gone tropo, as they say, off the wire, across the river and into the trees?

An envelope landed on the table in front of me amid the deafening din. I bolted from my chair and turned, scanning the drunken, sunburnt faces for clues to who might have made the drop. There were about a hundred immediate possibilities.

Opening the envelope, I found a single Polaroid head and torso shot of Nash bound and gagged with duct tape. Around her neck was a thin silver noose. She did not look happy. Someone out of frame held a mechanical device the size of a flashlight attached to the garrote. I turned the photo over. Scrawled on back, in an unfamiliar but impatient hand, was the message: "Hemingway House. You have 10 min."

I blew out of Sloppy's like a frat boy's lunch and sprinted around to Simonton, where I'd parked the Jeep. I unstrapped the Walther from beneath the driver's seat, checked the clip and wedged it into the back of my outriggers. They were uncomfortably snug with the .45 already lodged up front.

I hurried on foot to Eaton, then made a right and crossed Duval to Whitehead, bracing for an ambush at every turn. None came, just the usual stream of vacationing humans to impede my progress. I slowed to a trot past the Green Parrot bar and geared down to a fast walk as I neared the wall surrounding the Hemingway property. One of Papa's fabled six-toed cats looked down at me, devoid of curiosity.

The first gate I tried was locked, visiting hours to the museum long over. The second was ajar. I slipped in, returned it to its precarious state, and drew my .45.

I ran up the porch steps and into the foyer, closing the ornate front door behind me. I paused to let my senses adjust to the unlit old Victorian. It'd been years since I toured the place on an elementary fieldtrip. I wasn't too clear then who the hell Hemingway was or why our class was being made to walk through his fancy abode. I remember being impressed by the size of it and the animal heads on the walls, the first I'd seen of that strange ritual. I told a naïve classmate that one of the mountings was a Key deer and she created quite a scene for our divertissement. The trophy heads took on a whole new meaning for me now.

Conch houses talk to you if you have the ears to listen. The wood has memory and feeling and a sense of purpose that some locals call justice and others call vengeance. There is sometimes a feeling of being tested when entering an old house, to see if you are worthy of welcome.

I put my hand on the banister and felt a presence upstairs. Then floorboards creaked as weight shifted overhead. I cautiously climbed, step by step. A muffled, struggling sound grew louder the closer I got. At the landing, my ears led me toward a bedroom to the right. I proceeded in a crouch down the short hallway, feeling prickly heat at my neck.

The door was cracked. I inched it open with my foot, kneeling to make a smaller target of myself.

A dim green-shaded reading lamp snapped on across the room. I could see the whites of Loo's eyes and the strip of dull gray tape across her mouth. The shadowy figure of Ernest Hemingway loomed in the darkness behind her.

"What do you think of my aim now, Mr. Dodge?" came the first words I'd heard from Papa, a voice both surprisingly refined and familiar in a way I could not place. The shadow figure flicked the small hand unit to life, a very efficient-sounding motor. We had all seen what it was capable of.

I laughed. That manners thing again.

"I'd say you've lassoed yourself the wrong doggie there, Tex. She's got nothing to do with this."

"On the contrary, I believe she's your backup? That is what you call it, in your little cops and robbers world, isn't it? I would gladly have roped you in first, but this way will do nicely now."

"Can you operate that gadget without your head?" I wondered, speaking for my .45.

His turn to laugh.

"And an apt question of a self-beheaded author. Very good, Mr. Dodge. I am pleased you appreciate my little touches of irony. But to answer your question, should I let go of this, involuntarily let's just say, it will not stop until it has completed its job, which it does quite expeditiously, I might add. It has something to do with dynamic tension, all very technical. Still, you pay extra for the little things, it's human nature to want to use them, don't you think?"

He revved the motor for emphasis.

"I don't know, Ern. You didn't really get your money's worth from that quiet little gun of yours, did you? I mean it took Everett to finally win you a teddy bear."

"Yes. So unfortunate about Mr. Michaels. An innocent bystander, really."

"So's the girl. Let her go."

"I'm afraid that won't be possible, Mr. Dodge. We have gotten to know each other rather too well these past few hours. Haven't we, Sarah?"

The gist of her profane response was quite clear, despite the duct tape.

"Feel free to point your firearm at me if you like, but I would encourage you not to use it. For Sarah's sake."

I stepped to my right, inside the room, the .45 trained on his thorax. Neon from the continuous party on Duval Street pulsated off the darkened walls of the study.

"Where did it all start going south, Ern? Marty grow tired of your rigging?"

"Hmm. Amusing image, that, Marty ever growing tired of it. I doubt even the afterlife has had that effect on her. No, I'm sorry to say our party girl was insatiable in more ways than one. A shame really. She was such a broad-minded girl."

"So it was the money." I hadn't expected to have that conversation with the boy-toy.

He laughed again.

"This all must seem very confusing for you, Mr. Dodge. Believe me, I sympathize. In the beginning, things were very simple, an opportunity for all parties to fulfill their dreams. Marty wanted the moon, of course. That was Marty. She made a very nice living doing things she enjoyed doing anyway. Mr. Moony was paid handsomely for his rather limited abilities. And Everett, well, he was lifted up from the gutter and escorted into a virtual palace of earthly delights, a Bahamian's dream come true."

"And you got yours," I added.

"Crudely put but yes, I was not left wanting."

"So everybody's making Marty and making money. Where's the hitch, Ern?"

"Marty, in a word. Marty was the hitch. You take a hundred girls like Marty, from her walk of life, and present them with the same opportunity, they would do anything for you. But Marty had to have more and she thought she'd found a way to get it by blackmailing me. I agreed, at first. I would do anything for her. But we both knew it would never have been enough. Not for Marty."

"Blackmailing you? Why? You married? Family dough?"

"I'm afraid we must save that for another time, or in your case, another life, Mr. Dodge. Had you followed our eager Mr. Michaels down the path of least resistance, you would already be basking in the glory of another case solved and there would be no need for this…unpleasantness."

"And Everett Danswaller would be dimming the lights at Raiford," I said, raising my aim to his head. "Tell me, Ern, are you really ready to blow this planet just to kill my friend?"

His laugh was beginning to grate on me.

"Most certainly not. And now I believe it's time to take Mr. Dodge's plaything away. Jen?"

I saw Nash's eyes widen too late. Blunt steel gouged into the base of my skull. A familiar hand reached around me. I released the .45.

"Sorry, Jack," Jen whispered, close and warm against my ear.

I wanted to believe her. Somehow having my wrists bound behind me with duct tape made it harder.

"You may sit, Mr. Dodge. Jen?"

She lowered my brainpan into a wingback chair and stepped clear of me, toward the door. I looked into her deep blues. They were hiding scared behind her own fake beard and silver curls. I could still feel the pleasant pain where her skate blades had so recently scored my flanks. Now she held me at gunpoint, for reasons I probably would not live to learn.

"Look, Jen, maybe we should see other people," I offered.

"Don't fuck with this, Jack." She held the gun away from her like a snake. A .38 snake, by the looks of it.

"I'm just saying…"

"Quiet!" Papa revved his mojo threateningly. Nash closed her eyes, grimacing.

"Mr. Dodge, I'm afraid your colleagues will have to account for a couple more bodies now that we have concluded our discussion. Frankly, when I learned that Everett had failed me, I was stumped for an appropriate end for you. Then dear Sarah happened by and gave me the perfect idea, one I'm certain will meet with your approval. Everett was innocent, as you know. Your death can now vindicate him. And although we know you had nothing to do with the deaths of Marty or poor John, the evidence we will leave here tonight should indicate otherwise."

I calculated distances and counted my resources. I still had mobility. I still had the Walther. I still had a chance.

"The first step in this process is a most unpleasant one, I'm afraid," he said.

With the force of a sledgehammer blow, Papa struck Nash from behind, dropping her to the ground in one solid blow. I started to rise from my chair but Jen, shaken, motioned me back. On the floor next to Nash, flashing in the neon, lay a duck decoy, its head broken off.

"Easier on her this way," Papa explained, kneeling down to adjust the garrote.

Jen held fast on me, watching him in uneasy glances.

"Jen…" I said, trying to reach her.

"When they find my little device in your hand, Mr. Dodge, combined with the self-inflicted gunshot wound, a murder-suicide would be the logical conclusion, wouldn't you say?"

He knelt over Loo, one foot to her throat, a logger preparing to buck timber.

"Jen, for God's sake," I whispered.

I looked deep into her eyes, reaching for whatever humanity was left in her. Her eyes met mine, then raced back and forth between the killer and me.

"And so goodnight, my sleeping beauty," Papa said, revving the motor.

"NO!" Jen yelled, turning the gun suddenly on the bent figure. "No more! You said after Ev, no more!"

Papa exhaled impatiently and looked up. "I know what I said, Jen, but you understand there's no choice here, don't you? Just these two and everything returns to normal. You see that?"

"No! No more fucking bodies! No more fucking blood!"

"Would you prefer I use the flash pot? It worked well in John's case."

She was shaking now, eyes wide, washed with angry tears. She held the unsteady gun on him with both hands, stealing glances at me, did I want some. I did not.

He flicked the motor off and set it on Loo's chest, then stood up slowly, steepling his hands at his bearded mouth in thought.

"Jen, have I asked you to be a part in any of this? No. It was mine to deal with and I accepted that and went forward."

He stepped casually toward her, as if to correct her golf swing. She moved back, uncertain, the distance between the gun and Papa becoming less and less comfortable.

"Everett was not supposed to die, once I found him and we reached our new understanding. You know that. But Mr. Dodge here is a cat with many lives, apparently."

He slowed his steps as he approached her, casually placing a hand in the pocket of his khakis.

"No…more!" she hissed.

Her last words.

I heard the switchblade release a split second before I saw the swift underarm arc from his body to hers. She inhaled sharply, then the sound turned guttural as his bloody blade withdrew, having completed its mortal mission. The air escaped from her in a spray of red.

In the same moment, I kicked up from my chair, dove sideways, awkwardly aimed the Walther at Papa and fired, again and again, my shoulder crashing against the floor. A window blew out, then wood, followed by the muted, meaty thud of tissue impact.

Hurried footsteps raced out of the room and down the stairs.

I tucked the burning steel of the Walther into my back pocket, cut myself free against the window glass and hurried to Nash. She was unconscious but breathing. I carefully removed the garrote.

I knelt and turned Jen over in my arms. She was conscious, the free flow of scarlet already relaxing her features in preparation for death. I removed her Hemingway getup. She smiled up at me, sharing the Big Joke.

"You…got a smoke, Jack?"

I lit one from my pack and held it to her lips in the neon dark. The tip glowed. She inhaled. It sounded like bubbles.

"Domestic," she chided me.

"Yeah."

"We were good, Jack."

"Sure, kid."

One last drag.

"My sister…" and she laughed, then coughed.

I held her until she was gone.

I searched the half-light and found my .45; Papa had apparently grabbed the .38 from her falling hand in his flight. Then I knelt down and pulled on her Hemingway disguise. It was still warm and smelled like her, a smell I would never know again.

I proceeded carefully down the stairs, adjusting to the visual limitations of my new coiffure. The front door was wide open, as was the gate. He would attempt to disappear into the Papa Days pandemonium of Duval, I was certain of that. If I was lucky, he might only be looking over his shoulder for Jack Dodge.

I tucked the .45 into my waist and hurried out into the swift stream of tourists. Papa knew the rock well enough to know the alleys, but I sensed he would prefer the safety in numbers, having spent most of the week blending with the partiers. There were fewer tourists trudging toward the Atlantic end of Duval to my right. I crossed the street and headed left, toward the greater madness of Old Town.

I flew past the tee shirt shops and yogurt joints, stepping out to zigzag through traffic when the plaid shorts and socks crowd became gridlocked. The pulsating disco beat of the Epoch called to me as I passed. If he had ducked into a club, I was wrong about this guy. Dead wrong.

I squeezed my way through the geegawkers outside Ripley's Believe It or Not! Odditorium and slid past Barefoot Bob's, the Deadhead bar next door. I spent more time in the street than on the overflowing sidewalk the farther down Duval I ran. Cars honked, scooters beeped. I'd been called worse names, but not sober.

I got lucky when I neared Eaton and spotted a Hemingway clone, his beard darkened at the bottom, crossing against traffic. He turned and our eyes met. Recognizing either my shiner, my blood-stained clothes or my intent, he quickly disappeared upstream, against the crowd.

I slammed across hoods coming in both directions and drew my .45. I sprinted past the cattle herd outside Margaritaville and gained on him as the outrageous window displays of Fast Buck Freddie's flashed by to my left. He darted into the sundries store that locals use as a shortcut to the elevators serving the rooftop bar atop the seven-story La Concha Hotel. I burst through the store and into the interior corridor, wheeling around to the elevator just as the door closed. I pumped the button in vain, then took on the stairs, two at a time.

Couples stood at the railing of the open-air rooftop, drinking and marveling at the rock, lit up like an emerald in a jeweler's shop window. At the far end facing me stood Papa, pointing Jen's gun at me beneath his safari jacket, the side stained dark where I'd punched a leak.

Danswaller was right: I knew those eyes.

The sight of my gun sent several of the sightseers scurrying quickly toward the exit. It being Key Weird, a few turned to watch whatever was about to unfold, be it real, pretend, even hallucinatory.

"I'm a cop! Get inside. NOW!"

There were disappointed grumbles as they scattered.

"This island positively thrives on melodrama," Papa said.

"Throw down the gun, Ern," I said. "Or would you prefer Abby?"

The killer grinned. My arm hairs stood on end.

"You didn't know, did you?" He was almost gleeful.

"I knew it wasn't Moony because the killer tuned the radio in Marty's truck to disco. The physical description didn't fit Danswaller. The hairless arms in the porno shots had me stumped, but it makes sense now. The wonders of waxing, huh? When I heard your voice, I thought you were Abby impersonating a man. I didn't know the real deal until I watched you kill Jen."

"We weren't related, you know," he said, pulling off his soiled beard and white wig. "Except in the biblical sense, of course."

His face was the only thing about him that resembled the Abby I knew. His cool, cultured voice, his short dark hair, his wiry athletic build, even the intense intelligence behind those black eyes, all of it somehow had managed to disappear behind a most believably dour female facade.

"Why the charade? You just enjoy being a girl?"

"Let's say it makes my line of work easier, shall we?"

I laughed. "What line is that? Pornography?"

He chuckled. "A pastime. Merely a hobby. The real money is in hiding money, down here. I find it easier to do my business as the diminutive Abby Wilde than as myself. It keeps me disciplined and focused. And I must say, I do so love the cabaret aspect of it. And Father prefers the anonymity."

"The old man owns PNB Newsstand Services, I'm guessing."

"Among other tiresome holdings, yes, I'm afraid that is all too correct. Never go into the family business, Dodge. You'll never get out. At least this way I'm free to pursue, shall we say, my more creative self."

"So why kill Marty?"

"I got careless and did the unspeakable, I'm afraid. I fell in love. In doing so, I shared too much with her, including more of my true identity than Jen was comfortable with. She got angry, of course. Who wouldn't, with everything we'd set up, me behind the scenes, her out there working the P&B? When she couldn't drive Marty away, she tried to steal her from me. Anything to protect what we had. Marty was so wonderfully alive. A lot like me, I suppose, always wanting more. I had no choice but to eliminate her."

"By cutting her head off and screwing it?"

"To quote Rimbaud, 'The road of excess leads to the palace of wisdom'."

"Or the hot seat upstate," I said. "I should just drop you now."

"But you won't, Mr. Dodge. Code of the Old West and all that. Besides, part of you would secretly like to be me."

"Yeah, but we don't let him play with guns. Which brings me back to that one of yours."

I motioned with my wrist. He brought the .38 out of its hiding place and pointed it at me, waist high.

"Interesting situation, don't you agree, Mr. Dodge? All Hollywood climactic."

"Except for your aim. Now throw it down."

He fired instead. Wide right, again.

My first shot hit him just above the hip. He spun from the impact, then righted himself and fired again, overcompensating to the left. My second shot struck him in the midsection, in and up. The force threw him back against the railing. I saw the fabric from Marty's back brace through the rent in the khaki. I advanced slowly. He recovered his balance and leveled a final round at me, opening my ear again. The recoil and his leaks sent him slumping backward. I couldn't cover the distance between us in time as he toppled over the side.

I didn't bother to look.

Inside, the shaky bartender handed me a bar-rag full of ice for my ear and tried her best not to butcher my Manhattan. I carefully stripped off my beard and hairpiece. It must have looked worse underneath because she turned white as rice. I made her pour herself a shot of courage.

"Ear-shooters," I offered. Most of me even meant it.

Then Johnny's boys arrived.

Chapter 25
Luke

The Tallahassee twins honked and hollered farewells from their convertible as they flew by Smathers Beach to begin their long day's journey back home. Jonah sipped his Sunday mimosa from his strolling cup and watched wistfully as they disappeared into the sunrise. He was wearing his winged shades with the amethyst insets. And matching kimono, of course.

By the time I'd returned to the Hemingway place, Loo was up and already making a fuss about spending the night in observation at Fisherman's. The parameds overruled her. I didn't envy them that ride up-island to the hospital, but I would have liked to have seen the look on Limpin' Dick's face when she stormed in with the news. Pete, of course, would be doing the happy dance shortly.

The ER crew was the same bunch who'd stitched me up after my cemetery visit a few nights back. They put in a new seam, called me Vincent, made me a patch that looked like I'd lost half my earmuffs and filled my pockets with vitamin C-3.

A short time later, I was standing on the deck of Jen's stilt house, holding the last true blonde in my arms and watching the running lights from the charter boats as they cleared the jetty and headed out into the Gulf.

M. had turned. I knew it even before we'd boarded the good ship Medellin that cold December day. I knew it up in the Smokeys, as early as that. I think Pete knew it too, though he never spoke of it. Maybe he wonders if I know. There's the difference between us: Pete saves his energy for the living while I squander mine on the dead.

Ironically, the bureau never caught on. Hand it to M., she was that good. Unless you were in tactile contact with her, you wouldn't have noticed her body chemistry changing from alkaline to acid. But I knew her beyond well. We'd played these scenes through a hundred times, the two of us. She had tightened down too hard, letting the flake take over. The complete absence of signs was all the evidence I needed.

She died a hero. The bureau photo that doesn't look like her still hangs on their wall of honor or whatever it's called.

To this day, they don't know the half of it.

And now the memory of Jen will join hers, to haunt my days. Jen, who told me all she could, each time hoping it would be enough. Jen, who finally turned the right way, a little too late. Live fast, die young, leave a pretty corpse. She did.

She also left Lucien, aka Luke, my handsome parting gift and constant reminder of the Big Joke underlying all this. The past is gone, the future is uncertain. So it is written in the book of Luke. What we've got is right now. Smoke 'em if you got 'em.

Luke fell off the seawall for the umpteenth time.

Jonah did the honors, stooping down to gather in our blitheful little bundle of sand and fur. I seized the moment to light up. We wandered on down the strand, surveying this week's crop of nubile young women as they prepared their sun altars on this manufactured beach at the end of the road.

"So what *do* you get someone who's been shot by a crazed Bahamian Hemingway in a jet boat doing the bidding of a ruthless porno killer masquerading as a woman, hmm?" he asked me.

I drew a thoughtful drag and squinted out at the shrimpers working the Strait.

"A signed first edition might be nice."